# THUNDER
# IN
# THE
# NIGHT

## J.L. FREDRICK

Lovstad Publishing
Poynette, Wisconsin
Lovstadpublishing@live.com

ISBN: 0615745784
ISBN-13: 978-0615745787

First Edition

Printed in the United States of America

Cover design by Lovstad Publishing

For Charlie and Frenchy

Other Novels by J.L. Fredrick

The Great Train Robbery of Monroe County
Mad City Bust
September Ten
The Other End of the Tunnel
Across the Dead Line
Another Shade of Gray
Cursed by the Wind
Aftermath

Non-Fiction

Rivers, Roads, & Rails

# THUNDER
# IN
# THE
# NIGHT

# Summer, 1868

*H*e was grubby from the brown dust along the river trail and all around his bright blue eyes there were marks where his dirty fingers had rubbed away the tickling tears. The dust darkened his delicate white skin and matted his strawberry blond curls. But now the chubby little fingers of his hands seemed clean, as he was sitting on a bed of moss near the roadside where spring water came trickling down from the rocky cliff above, and he splashed in the tiny pool till the pearly drops hung in his curls like jewels and dotted the ragged old shirt, many sizes to large, that seemed to make up his only garment. The man-sized jersey hung on the boy of about three with its sleeves cut off at his elbows, and the very bottom torn off and made into a belt tied around the little guy's waist to keep the jersey from slipping off.

Rays of sunlight flashed upon the droplets in his hair and in the ferns, some drooping over the pool and some reaching up as high as the silvery-green foliage of the overhanging birch that fluttered delicately in the soft summer breeze. He laughed merrily when the water flew up into his face, and at the height of his enjoyment he threw back his head. Two rows of pearly white teeth flashed in the sunshine behind his parted lips. As dirty as he was, the water, ferns, moss and wild flowers around him seemed most delightful, and at that very moment he was supremely happy.

After a time he glanced downward; a frown wrinkled his forehead and his lips pursed. Dipping his hands in the clear water he rubbed the little fingers over and between his toes to get rid of the dust and grit. While the breeze whispered and the birch trees gently waved and the wildflowers nodded, from nearby came at regular intervals a low growl, like that of a wild beast.

And then there came the clop, clop, clop of horse's hooves and the rattle of wheels on the dusty road. A sleepy-looking gray mare pulling a green wagon came into sight. Aboard the wagon were a man and a woman, a farmer and his wife on their way into town for supplies. They approached slowly and would have passed by had the woman not caught a glimpse of the little boy and abruptly grabbed hold of her husband's arm and pointed. The man eased back on the reins to stop the horse, and they both stared open-mouthed at the youngster.

"Sakes alive, Isaac! Look at that," the woman said in a whisper, while the little guy continued to wash his toes.

"I'm a lookin' at him. Wonder where he belongs," the man replied. His face twisted into a silent little laugh, and then turned to a frown as his wife began to climb down from the wagon seat. "There... what d'ya think yer gonna do?"

"What a beautiful little boy, Isaac. He must be lost. We should—"

"We shouldn't do nothing," Isaac grumbled.

She was standing only a few feet from the boy. "Oh, Isaac, how I'd love to give him a good bath and dress him in clean clothes."

Isaac sat forward on the seat with his elbows on his

knees and continued to grumble. "Bath! He looks perfectly happy where he is. We don't go to market t' find lost children."

She approached the smiling boy slowly and stooped down to caress his golden curls, when a loud roar like that of a vicious beast sounded from a patch of tall grass just beyond the boy. The woman jumped back frightened; the horse jerked to one side; the farmer raised his whip and braced for trouble. They both stared at the grizzly-looking character that rose from the tall grass who had been sleeping, and was now glowering at them with folded arms. He was not a pleasant looking fellow by any means, scraggly beard and uncombed hair; his skin blotched with disease; his clothes soiled and foul.

"Ya leave th' young pup alone!" he growled, half closing his dark eyes.

Astonished more than frightened, the woman flinched. "Oh, Isaac," she gasped.

"Here now," the farmer said fiercely. "Don't you be frightening my wife like that! She was only tryin'—"

"Leave th' youngin alone," the man growled again.

"How did you come by the boy?" the woman asked, somewhat recovering her composure. "Certainly he is not yours."

"Not mine!" the man replied in his harsh voice. "Y' let him be, or I'll show ya 'bout that." He gently clapped his hands together. "Hey! Pup."

The little fellow scrambled to him, threw his tiny arms around the man's thick neck, nestled his head on the man's broad shoulder, and gazed at the farmer and his wife.

"Oh, my," whispered the woman, unable to break her stare at the unusual duo.

"Well? Whatcha lookin' at?" the man growled. "Ya didn't think th' pup was yours, now, did ya?"

It was quite clear to the farmer that the love and affection the boy displayed toward the man seemed genuine, and they must belong together, no matter how absurd it appeared. "Come along, Missus," he said in a stern tone. "We'll be on our way."

She reluctantly climbed aboard the wagon and took her seat beside the farmer. "It just don't seem right," she whispered to Isaac. "That he should have such a child as that."

"Well, it ain't none of our business now," he replied, clicked his tongue and snapped the whip at the horse's hind quarters. The gray mare responded immediately and the green wagon with the farmer and his wife went rattling down the road, but for as long as they were within sight, the farmer's wife stared back; she could not take her eyes off him. "The poor little boy," she thought.

And for as long as they were within sight, the rough-looking tramp glared at her from among the tall grass.

"Must be movin' on," he grumbled to himself several times as he attempted to get to his feet, but his joints seemed so stiff that he could only get to his knees, and he had to set the boy down. After quite a struggle, he managed to get standing upright, holding onto a birch branch to steady himself. He staggered to a large boulder and sat down. "Come here, pup," he growled. His tone of voice should have frightened a child away, but the little guy wasn't the least bit alarmed. He bounded to the tramp with outstretched arms and was grateful for the gnarled hands to pick him up. Then with a mighty swing the man threw the boy over his shoulder and onto his back, nearly losing his balance and barely saving himself from tumbling to the ground. He grumbled a bit, and the little burden uttered a whimpering cry.

"Hold on tight," the old man said, and almost instantly the little white arms were clinging around his neck, the hands hidden under the man's tangled beard. The man got to his feet again and together they ambled along the road.

The day and the miles passed. The sun beat down on the curly little head and the dust rose from the tramp's staggering steps. The cheery songs from the larks, the heat, and the motion finally lulled the boy to sleep. But he did not fall. It was a natural instinct that maintained his hold, so that he clung tightly to the man, who seemed almost oblivious to his existence.

The old tramp continued his deliberate but now faltering journey, often muttering incoherently about things that didn't make sense, even to himself. But even though his alertness was continually fading, more rapidly now than in the past few days, his awareness remained keen enough to know he must reach his destination, for the sake of the little one.

Then came the soft evening light when shadows grew long and the relentless summer heat eased its smothering grip, as the old man struggled along toward houses and the town. Groups of people he passed turned to stare at the coarse-looking creature, some with disgust, some with wonder, and others with grins and less-than-complimentary remarks. The man paid no attention to them and kept on his course, and continued the strange babbling, until he came to a marketplace that seemed familiar, but in his dazed condition he found himself confused and lost. He turned to one idle man standing near and uttered one word: "Mission."

"Beg your pardon?" the bystander replied, in awe that such an abomination of a man could be toting the likes of an innocent, sweet child.

"Th' Mission," the tramp growled again fiercely.

"Oh!" was the response. Now it seemed clear that this derelict was seeking help. He pointed toward the bluffs. "That way... about a half-mile."

The old tramp staggered on his way, but by now his progress had been slowed even more, and by the time he reached the entrance of the familiar stone building, darkness was swallowing everything in sight. His feeble pounding on the wooden door gained no response. Then he remembered the rope hanging beside the doorway, gave a little tug, and heard the bell.

Moments later, the door opened revealing the strange pair to a middle-aged woman, who at first observed nothing more than an unkempt, repulsive harlot. And then from behind the mass of dirty, tangled hair a smiling little face peeked over his right shoulder.

"Me li'l pup... he needs you," the man whispered.

In an instant, the woman's experienced eyes read the urgency, and she took the tramp's arm, steadying him as she ushered him through the doorway.

## *Chapter 2*

*T*he doctor shook his head hopelessly as he looked down at the old tramp lying on a straw tick, mumbling painfully. Mr. Stanley, master of the Mission School, and a couple of his able assistants stood by watching when there was a loud cry from the little boy as the woman who had brought the pair in, took the youngster from where he was seated at the foot of the bed and carried him toward the door. In the next moment, the sick old man sprang up in the bed, glaring wildly and stretching out his arms. He was trying to say something, but the words just wouldn't form.

"Quickly! Take the boy away," said Stanley, but the doctor held up his hand, as if to order silence, all the while watching the sick old man. He whispered to Stanley a few words, who then gave a reluctant consent for the boy to be placed back on the bed within the old man's reach, and when their hands touched, the old man vented a sigh of relief and sank his head into the pillow again. The child nestled to his side, sobbing, but he, too, soon calmed down.

Mr. Stanley approached the doctor. "Seems to be against all the rules," he said in an ill-tempered tone.

"Yes, indeed it is, Mr. Stanley," replied the doctor. "But it will do more good than anything I can do for him." The doctor put his hand on Stanley's shoulder. "Trust me... it

7

won't be for long."

Stanley nodded.

"Mrs. Champlain," the doctor went on. "You can sit with him tonight?"

"Yes, sir," the woman answered. "I can watch him."

"Keep an eye on the boy, in case the old man turns violent," the doctor said. "But I don't think he will."

"And if he does, shall I send for you, Doctor?"

"Yes, by all means. But I don't think he will."

Mr. Stanley turned to her. "You might want to light a fire in the stove if you'd like some tea. And I'll send in some food for you, and milk for the boy."

The doctor and the others left the infirmary, and then Mrs. Champlain settled in for the long night watch. All was very still in the whitewashed room until one of Stanley's assistants brought in a platter of bread, butter, cheese, and a small jar filled with milk. The little boy hungrily ate the bread and butter and cheese that Mrs. Champlain gave him, and sat quietly on the bed, smiling and contented. The only sounds that broke the silence were the occasional mutterings from the sick old man. But that didn't seem to disturb the boy. He finished the bread, drank some of the milk, and then sank into the mattress at the foot of the bed. A short while later he was fast asleep.

The night was comfortably warm, so Mrs. Champlain didn't see the need to cover him. From time to time as the long hours passed, she went to the bed and wiped the sick old man's forehead with a cool, wet cloth, giving him what little comfort she could offer. And then she would stop at the foot of the bed and gently stroke the boy's golden hair with her fingers. Once, the boy gave out a little giggle, still deep in slumber. The woman wiped the corners of her eyes with her apron, and then bent down and kissed his cheek.

The clock in the main hall chimed by the hours, and just past midnight, she slipped into a dream while sitting in her comfortable padded chair. It was a pleasant dream, where she was young again, and her own son who never returned from the war in the south was young again, and they were strolling together through a fragrant meadow with bountiful wildflowers, and scores of beautiful song birds... and a clock's bell that chimed six times. She awoke, startled.

"Oh dear me," she said softly. "I must've dozed off." She gazed at the little boy resting so peacefully. *What a beautiful child* she thought, and then she went to the old man once more with the wet cloth. But as she wiped his forehead this time, she realized that it would be of little use.

Mrs. Champlain quickly swept up the sleeping boy in her arms and hurried out of the room, down the hallway to her own quarters where she laid him on her bed.

About an hour later, he awoke. "Papa!" he cried, wanting to go to the tramp. But there was no tramp for him to go to. During the night, the rough old man had left on a journey where he could not take the boy. As if he had lost his last hope, the boy cried bitterly until the woman returned from the rather unpleasant tasks in the infirmary. Her gentle voice and some more bread and butter and milk seemed to sooth the boy. He liked her, and because of the kindness and warmth she had offered him the night before, she had at once become the next person he would cling to. He offered no objection to be bathed.

"Yes, sir," Mrs. Champlain explained to the doctor. "Went off quiet in his sleep."

"And the boy?" the doctor asked.

"He cried," Mrs. Champlain replied "But I fed him and gave him a good warm bath this morning, which he desperately needed."

"Poor little waif," the doctor mumbled as he left the room with Stanley. "A tramp's child, cast out with nothing but a dirty shirt covering his back."

Mrs. Champlain called to him: "He'll be okay, you can be sure. We'll take good care of him."

"You see, Stanley?" the doctor said. "I was right. It wasn't for long."

.

# Chapter 3
## Barron's Island; May 1877

*T*he cabin door opened slowly. A tousled round head of dark hair appeared. The boy's sleepy face turned downward, eyes adjusting to the morning light, then gradually lifted to meet the new day. It seemed to catch the magic of that May morning, brightening like a chalice filling with sunshine. The door swung wider, framing the boy's eager figure, poised as if for flight.

The sun would soon peek over the hills on the other side of the river, but it seemed as though no one else was stirring at this early hour. With motion as light as a dove the boy darted from the step to the footpath that curved toward the beach, his moccasin clad feet scarcely touching the pebbles as he raced past the gardens and the apple trees now laden with fragrant white blossoms. Every muscle in his body strained with the joy of young strength and speed. So swiftly he ran that he almost took wing with the gulls that soared up from his path, and he was gone so quickly that the sleeping dogs barely had time to rise with a quick, savage bark, sniffing the air, not knowing that it was more than a spring wind that had brushed past them.

Finally, Dominic stopped, out of breath. He had run as far as he could without plunging into the river at North Point. He looked back along the shore that curved in a crescent, holding the west edge of the basin where three rivers mingled their waters to become one. Directly across the basin, the La Crosse River flowed from among the hills in the east, and from the north, the Black River opened its mouth wide to accommodate the shipyards and mills, and both contributed to the majesty of the mighty Mississippi that, to Dominic, stretched immeasurably.

His gaze followed the streets of La Crosse on the opposite bank of the river. In the evening sun, the houses there were stained with golden light from the setting sun, but now they were bathed in the grayness of a hazy dawn. His own little village that was known only as Barron's Island would soon feel the warmth of the morning sun, long before the city would creep out from the shadows of the great bluffs behind it. This had all been sacred ground to his mother's people at one time, where tribal gatherings and ceremonies were held, and where games of skill were played on the broad sandy prairie, and where friendship was celebrated among the various tribes regularly. But now it all belonged to the pioneers of the new nation, and Dominic had only the memory of his mother and her stories of how life had once been.

The sun was high above the eastern bluffs when to the northwest, from where the silvery Mississippi meandered down the vast valley it had carved in ancient times, Dominic spotted a familiar sight. Tall twin stacks billowing black-brown smoke appeared just above the treetops, and the baritone hiss of a distant steam whistle echoing between the hills announced the approaching vessel. Perhaps it was just another raft boat bringing a giant raft of logs down from the Chippewa. Or, it could be a packet—the Phil Sheridan, perhaps—on which his father and two older half-brothers would be returning. He raced back to the cabin with wild anticipation. There he would launch his canoe in the lagoon and paddle out to the river, across the basin to the boatyard and the wharfs where all the packet boats docked for passengers and freight. If his father and brothers did not arrive, he could still spend a portion of the day among his boatyard friends. The wharf laborers, mill workers, log rafters, and boat crews all knew him and had become accustomed to his presence there. They had learned to admire his simple-natured qualities, always happy and smiling, but appearing rather unkempt and perhaps neglected, although he never spoke of family to anyone on the docks. His speech indicated French heritage, but his skin was bronze and his hair was dark, suggesting that some native blood ran through his veins. Despite his outward appearances, though, almost everyone on the riverfront adored "Frenchy," as was the only name by which they knew him, and regarded him with a mixture of amusement, affection and respect.

His father and brothers did not arrive that morning, nor did they arrive on any other steamboats that stopped at the La Crosse wharf that day. Near sundown, Dominic put his string of sunfish that he had caught fishing from the pier into his canoe and paddled home. Once again he would eat his supper alone, and go to bed in a lonely house.

It was a fine house, built of logs and chinked with clay, topped with a cedar roof. Facing the river were parlor and dining room. On the island lagoon side were bedroom and kitchen, and a small bedroom had been added for Dominic and his half-brothers. And just to the north, fifty feet away, stood the little log storehouse, mostly empty now, but it would soon contain the wares of which his father made his business.

He lay there that night, unable to fall asleep, gazing out at the stars. A wave of reminiscent love washed over him, followed by a sharp pang of hurt as he envisioned the small headstone in the churchyard bearing the name Felicia Marie Bouton. That name had been given to his mother by Father LeClaire just after Dominic was born. But he knew that she was an Indian woman, and in his heart she would always be Morning Star, the beautiful daughter of a Winnebago chief.

About midnight, Dominic drifted off to asleep.

## *Chapter 4*

*E*arly the next morning he awoke with a start. Three days a week, all spring, summer, and fall, several residents of La Crosse hired him to take their cows to pasture and watch the herd all day while they grazed in the green grassy slopes beneath the bluffs. Today was his day, and by the time the sun was up over the high bluffs, everyone was usually done with the milking chores, and the cows were anxious to get out of the little city barns and out into the open meadow. His pay was forty cents per day, and a quart of chilled milk.

He finished his breakfast of salt pork and bread, and paddled out of the lagoon to the river just as the sun broke through the trees that lined the top of Granddad's Bluff. Learning the skills of paddling and maneuvering a canoe at the age of six from his mother's brother, Gray Wolf, Frenchy was as expert at slicing through the water as any man, and he made quick work of crossing the channel with little effort. He landed below Front Street at Pearl, just across from the Western Enterprise Hotel. Mr. Kellogg, the hotel owner always kept an eye on Frenchy's canoe for him while he tended the cows, one of which was Mr. Kellogg's, and Mr. Kellogg was the one who collected from the other cow owners and paid Frenchy each week. He doled out the quarts of milk, too, but he rarely kept track of how much milk had been dispensed to the boy. He adored Frenchy as much as anyone else in the town.

Frenchy made his usual route across town, leading each cow from its barn, tethering the beasts' halters to a centrally located fence rail until he had gathered all eight animals, and then untied them and drove them a mile or more to the pasture land beyond the reaches of the city.

All day he watched from the higher ground over the rooftops of the town to the sparkling river as the steamboats came and went. He wondered if one of them had deposited his father and brothers at the wharf, and if they would be waiting for him when he got home. And he wondered what present his father would have for him, as he usually did when he returned from a long voyage.

As the sun crept nearer the western horizon, Frenchy heard the church bells in town chiming six o'clock. He rounded up all the cows and headed them down the slope toward the city. Getting them back home was usually quite easy; the cows knew it was almost time for the evening milking, and each one seemed to know its way back to its own little barn without any prodding. When all the cows were safely returned home, Frenchy ran to the back door of the Western Enterprise Hotel where he collected his jar of milk from Mr. Kellogg, and then hurried across the channel to Barron's Island.

But his father's bateau was not tied up in the lagoon, and no one was waiting in the house to greet him.

On his next day in the bluff meadow tending the cows, he thought a lot about his father and brothers. Henri Bouton, his father, the proud French-Canadian had, for many years, been a trader on the island, and even when the town across the river grew to larger proportions, Henri stayed and remained faithful to the few friendly Winnebago Indians who still dwelled among the near hills. That's how he had met his wife, the mother of Dominic, when the untimely death of his first wife left him in a world of grief; she drowned in the river during a raging spring flood, and it wasn't only her death that had troubled Henri: she was with child when she died.

Then Morning Star came into his life. The beautiful Indian maiden agreed to stay after the autumn trading festivities were over, to help Henri care for his two young sons. Exposing her to the more comfortable, luxurious lifestyle of the French trader, she soon fell in love with Henri, and he took her as his wife. A year later, Dominic was born, and Morning Star was christened with her new French name, Felicia Marie.

Eight more years passed. Although he was raised in strong French culture because his father would have it no other way, Dominic secretly admired the Indian side of his heritage, as well. Dominic grew strong, influenced by his mother's family who visited frequently, learning about nature, hunting skills, canoeing and survival from his uncle, Gray Wolf. He savored every moment when his Indian uncles and cousins came to camp on the island during the trading festivals, and he listened intently when his mother told him the stories of her ancestors who had long ago made this wonderful valley their home.

Tragedy knows no mercy. Felicia Marie—Morning

Star—fell ill with a fever that no doctor could cure. After a week of torturous misery, she joined her ancestors in the Great Beyond. Her body was laid to rest in the churchyard, next to the grave of Henri's first wife, because that's the way he wanted it.

Now, the memory of her beautiful brown eyes and her flowing black hair haunted Frenchy's dreams. He missed her warm smiles and her motherly touch. He thought about her often, and he found it difficult to understand why his father didn't seem to miss her at all anymore.

And then there were his two older half brothers, Jacques and Louis. They had never felt any close devotion to Morning Star, even though she tried her best to love them as if they were her own. To them she was merely a nanny who prepared their food, washed and mended their clothes, and tucked them into bed at night. But they, too, had suffered a tragic loss when their mother died, so they understood Dominic's painful sorrow, and they had been a great comfort to him at a time when he needed to be close to someone.

Now they were older. Jacques was eighteen, and he was preparing to venture into the western wilderness, to follow in his father's footsteps as a trader. He had been a devoted apprentice, and he was now well acquainted with all his father's business associates in Montreal, as he had accompanied Henri to the Canadian city several times. Soon he would establish his own trade network somewhere in the vast, unsettled west. His diligence promised him a successful future.

Sixteen-year-old Louis had made his choice for the future, as well, and for quite some time, Henri had been determined to ensure his son's acceptance into Montreal

College, so that he may enter the Seminary of St. Sulpice to study for the priesthood. He wanted nothing else but to become a missionary for God.

Dominic admired his older brothers, and although he thought he would miss not having them close, he felt a peculiar happiness for them, that they were achieving what they wanted most. But it had not occurred to him, yet, that his lack of enthusiasm to pursue such professional levels was one of the reasons his father did not coddle him, as was the case with his other two sons. But Dominic was about to learn that lesson very soon.

## Chapter 5

*T*he church bells in town chimed six o'clock, and it was time to drive his herd back to their little city barns for milking. After he had collected his jar of milk from Mr. Kellogg, Dominic rushed to his canoe. Something in his heart told him that today his father and brothers would be waiting for him.

Joy danced in his big brown eyes when he spotted the bateau loaded with wooden crates tied at the bank of the lagoon. He wasted little time in dragging his canoe aground, and then ran to the house carrying the milk. There, around the plain pine table, polished by daily rubbing by many elbows, sat Henri Bouton and his two sons, Jacques and Louis, each sipping from wine glasses, the bottle at the table's center. When the door flew open and Dominic appeared, they all jumped to their feet. Louis reached the boy first and laid his hands on Dominic's shoulders. "Bless you, my brother," he said. "It is so good to see you again!"

Then Jacques, much taller and stronger, wrapped his arms around Dominic's middle, hoisted him up, and kissed the boy's cheek. "How is mon frère petit? Eh?" Jacques laughed.

Dominic still held the milk in one hand, but he managed to return the hug with sincere affection. "Bien, bien!" he replied. "I am ever so good! And I am ever so happy to see you have returned safely."

Henri grabbed the milk jar from Dominic's grasp, set it on the table, and then took the boy in his arms. "Ahh, *bonjour mon fils,*" he said, squeezing the boy tightly.

"*Bonjour, M'sieur* my Father. Did you have a good voyage? What kept you so long? You are three days late coming home."

"Good voyage? *Oui,*" said Henri. "*Je suis désolé...* I'm sorry for being late. We were delayed visiting mon ami Monsieur Cousteau... in Milwaukee."

"Milwaukee?"

"Oui," Henri replied. "And we just arrived late this afternoon by train." He looked the boy up and down. "You have been tending the cattle today?"

"Oui, M'sieur. I have milk for our supper." He gazed around, puzzled, thinking he had somehow lost the milk. Then he saw the jar on the table and beamed a smile, proud that he could help provide for his family. He looked around again curiously. "Did you bring me a present?"

"Present? Did I not promise you a present?" Henri released the boy to his feet, reached into a carpet bag next to the table, and presented a fancy wooden box with a hinged cover, six inches square, handsomely varnished, and a colorful three-mast sailing ship painted on the top. The brass hinges squeaked just a little as Dominic lifted the cover. Inside were several compartments containing a spool of very thin but strong fish line, and hooks of various sizes. Dominic's small fingers caressed the shiny hooks.

"Do you like?" asked Henri.

Dominic's eyes shone with appreciation. "*Oui! Merveilleux!* Yes, it is wonderful. *Merci!* Thank you! He hugged his father's neck.

"I have a present for you, too, *frère petit,*" said Jacques,

21

retrieving the gift from his bag. He held it out in offering to his "frère petit"—his little brother. It, too, was another attractive wooden box, a foot long and narrow. Birds on the wing decorated the top.

Dominic gently took the box from his brother's hand and carefully removed the cover, not knowing what to expect. On the pillowed lining of red velvet lay an exquisite flute, ornately carved of hard wood and polished to a mirror-like finish, little gold rings inserted around all the finger holes. He didn't touch it; he just stared at it in amazement. Then he glanced up at Jacques with a puzzled look in his eyes.

"I haven't heard you play the flute that your uncle made for you in a long time," Jacques said. "Louis and I thought this might get you started again."

It was true. Dominic hadn't played that flute in nearly a year. Morning Star had taught him to play that simple instrument handmade by Gray Wolf from a willow branch. It was old and dry and cracked, and was unlikely to produce any sound at all now. But at one time, he could out-sing the birds with at least a dozen different melodies.

"Go ahead," Jacques said. "Try it."

Reluctantly, Dominic picked the flute from its velvet bed, positioned his fingers along the tube, and slowly brought the mouthpiece to his lips. He was amazed at the richness of tone the flute emitted as he simply played up and down the scale. He paused and grinned at Jacques, and then he played a soft, happy little lullaby tune—the first one he had ever learned. It wasn't perfect, but it *had* been a long time since he played. As he finished, Jacques, Louis and Henri all applauded his talent.

"Magnifique! Magnifique!" his father shouted. "Now

you can serenade the cows out on the hillside."

After they ate their supper of venison and wild rice—and milk—the conversation continued about the voyage just completed to Montreal. Henri told of his experiences bargaining with all the warehouse owners, and all the fine dinner parties he attended as a guest of some of the wealthiest businessmen in Montreal. "And you know, Dominic," he said. "They were quite impressed with Jacques, and they will see to it that he will be very successful as a merchant in the west."

Dominic grinned a congratulatory smile at his oldest brother. Jacques had always been kind to him and treated him well, and he deserved to become successful. Jacques smiled warmly back at him.

"And there is good news about Louis, too," Henri said proudly. "This year he will begin his studies at Montreal College, and then perhaps next year, Louis will enter the Seminary."

Dominic smiled at Louis, but what he saw in return from the future scholar was what he thought to be a sneer.

"What about me, M'sieur?" Dominic asked his father. "When will it be time for me to go on a voyage with you to Montreal?"

Henri gave a hearty laugh. "Listen to *mon petit*... my little one!" he said laughing some more. "Dominic... the lazy one, who only wishes to while away his days watching cattle eat grass on the hillside. If I were to take you to Montreal, I should have to leave you in the bateau, covered with a tarpaulin, so that no one there would see what Henri Bouton fathered in the wilderness. *Bois Brulé*... that's what you are."

"I'm not *Burnt Wood!*" cried Dominic.

"Father," Jacques intervened. "I don't wish to be disrespectful, but *mon frère petit* did not get to choose the color of his skin. And he is but a child. Certainly he has not yet had time to decide on a profession."

"Look at him, Jacques," said his father. "He is a hunter... like his Indian cousins. A merchant he will never be."

*"Mon Pére,"* Dominic addressed his father. "It is true... I do not wish to be a merchant." He moved close to Jacques and leaned heavily against his brother. "I wish to stay here in the sacred valley and grow crops and raise cattle. I want to become a farmer."

"There! You see?" said Jacques. "Mon frère petit *has* chosen a profession." He put his arm around Dominic's shoulders and smiled.

# Chapter 6

*T*he next morning Dominic woke early and instead of making his breakfast, he wanted to be on his way to tend the cows before his brothers and father rose from their beds. He carefully and quietly put a chunk of bread and some cheese in his deerskin pouch that already held his new flute, slung the long strap over his shoulder and silently whisked out the door to his waiting canoe.

While he sat on the shady slope watching the cows meander about, sampling the grass here and there until each one finally settled into its choice spot, he nibbled on his bread and cheese. He imagined that on Barron's Island his father, Jacques, and Louis were busy unloading the crates of merchandise from the barge into the storehouse, unpacking them and arranging the wares so that all were displayed on the shelves and tables. He wondered if he had made a mistake by telling his father that he didn't want to be a merchant, and that his interests rather were in farming. Even he realized that he was still too young to understand what his life's ambition should be. "But here is where I will always be," he said. "Let Jacques go off to the far west to become a trader in Father's footsteps. Let Louis travel from mission to far mission as a priest. But *this* is where I belong."

The long sunlit hours passed slowly. Dominic lay back on the green hillside. Behind closed eyelids visions of the valley floated in a hazy warm blur. What a good, peaceful moment this was, and yet, he would like to be roaming the countryside. Not long ago he had seen a loon's nest at the edge of a little inlet. Wild flowers were springing up from the deep dark floors of the forest. Swallows glided and swooped about the rocky bluff's shaded crevices.

Then his thoughts began to fade and the tinkling of the cowbells came only faintly to his senses. On the lap of this glorious valley, he drifted off into a restful nap.

He awoke with hunger. His slight breakfast had not been enough. The sun was still high; it was a long time until supper, and with each passing minute he grew more and more hungry. Finally, in desperation, he knelt at the udder of one of the cows and gently squeezed spurts of milk into his mouth. Not until his fingers were tired and the bossy moved away in search of more grass did he stop. But he felt much better.

Dominic sat down in the grass next to a large boulder that had long ago rolled down from the bluff and leaned against it. He took the flute from the leather bag, admired it for a few moments, and then started practicing some of the songs his mother had taught him. The angelic sounds drifted over the valley, and somewhere there was probably a pair of ears that heard, and recognized the Indian compositions, and perhaps thought Morning Star's spirit had returned to earth.

At six o'clock, the cows were anxious to go home, and Dominic was anxious to collect for his week's work from Mr. Kellogg.

# *Chapter 7*

*H*enri and Jacques were busy early the next morning preparing for the trading festival. Barron's Island would soon be encamped by Winnebago Indians, tribes from Wisconsin, Minnesota, and Iowa. They came to trade their handcrafted goods and produce and pelts for Henri Bouton's wares—pots and pans, cutlery and utensils, fabrics, thread, needles, buttons, rope, tools, garden seeds, hats—the list went on and on. Henri had always treated them fairly, and they remained loyal to their French trader friend.

Dominic waited at North Point. His uncle and cousin would be among the group coming up the Mississippi from Iowa. He eagerly anticipated their arrival as he had not seen them since last year. True to tradition, his uncle, Gray Wolf, had taught him so many things, and his cousin, Silver Cloud, had always been a wonderful playmate. But they didn't come for visits as often as they once had. Now, it was only during the trading festivals that they camped on Barron's Island, perhaps, Dominic thought, because he was old enough now, and he didn't need as much guidance. Or maybe it was because Morning Star was gone. She had been the real connection to her brother. Dominic didn't let any of that bother him now, and he so looked forward to their visit; four days and nights would offer plenty of time for him and Silver Cloud to do all the things they usually did: target shooting with bow and arrow; fishing; hiking; swimming. And there would be words of wisdom from Gray Wolf in the light of the campfire at night, and stories, and songs, and now Dominic could entertain too, with his new flute. Oh, how he hoped he could play for them!

Then he saw the flash of sunlight reflecting off the canoe paddles as the small fleet rounded the bend in the river, skimming through the silvery ripples, graceful as gulls and brilliant as butterflies, the canoes long and slender like willow leaves. As they drew near, Dominic could see the painted feathers and the colorful blankets and the silver ornaments gleaming in the morning sun.

Now there were others from the little village gathered on the shore watching the arrival of the travelers; it was always a grand event. Dominic peeled off his clothes and plunged into the water as naked as the day he was born. Those watching from the beach saw him swimming rapidly out to meet the approaching canoes, and then he suddenly vanished. The Indians in the canoes laughed and shouted. "He covers himself as with a blanket!" Their wide-eyed glances darted about over the empty surface, but Gray Wolf knew his trick. Silver Cloud had taught the boy to swim under water, like an otter, and he would come up where he was least expected.

Then a clamor of whoops and yells came from the canoes; there was Dominic, spouting water, dodging the paddles, and then turning to race the fleet to the shore. The dogs barked and the Winnebago laughed and cheered, delighted to have such a spectacular welcome.

All of them knew Dominic. They came from his mother's native village, twenty miles downriver, and some were his kin. To them, this journey was a holiday as well as an opportunity for trade. Their canoes were piled with pelts, beautiful woven mats and baskets, moccasins, bags of wild rice and dried corn, clay jars filled with hominy, maple sugar, and wild honey.

Having pulled the boats ashore there was a great flurry as the new arrivals set up their portable tepees and arranged all their possessions. But for the moment, Dominic was only interested in his uncle and cousin. He had pulled on his clothes and they sat talking as Gray Wolf waited for the others to get located. He was representing his father, Chief Red Hawk, so his lodge was to stand a little apart.

"How long will you stay on the island?" Dominic asked.

The Indian's hardened face wrinkled as he looked down at the boy. He suspected that Dominic was looking forward to many days of companionship—hiking and hunting, and absorbing new knowledge and skills from his uncle, and perhaps some recreational time with his cousin. "When three moons have passed," he said, "We must journey back down the river."

Three days wasn't nearly as long as they had stayed in the past, but Dominic didn't feel disappointed; he was glad that he had this time to spend with his Indian relatives.

Gray Wolf gazed around the camp; it appeared that all the others in the party had their tepees located. "Now I must prepare our lodge." He motioned to his son, Silver Cloud.

"May I help you?" Dominic asked eagerly, and his uncle nodded.

The boy was supremely happy as he assisted them to raise and fasten the lodge poles, unpack and stretch the skins over the framework. And when the mats were all spread and a small fire lit with an iron cooking pot hung over it, Dominic surveyed it all with pride. An unidentifiable longing swelled up inside him. "I wish I could share your lodge all the while you are here," he said.

The old Indian laid his hand on Dominic's shoulder. "My lodge is poor and simple, Little Otter. It is not rich with feather beds and glass oil lamps and brass kettles. It is not good enough to honor the son of the French Trader. But later we will hunt, and tomorrow we will feast together. We shall have a good day, you, and I, and Silver Cloud."

That night, after a long afternoon of hunting rabbits on the far side of the island with bow and arrow, Dominic bid his father the customary good-night: "Bon soir, M'sieur," and then turned to go to his bed. Suddenly an arrow of fear pierced his happiness. Framed in the darkness of a far window was a shadowy face—an Indian face, proud and fierce, eyes burning with a secret, menacing stare, unmistakable to Dominic.

Dominic quickly turned his gaze away and forced himself to quietly walk to Jacques. He leaned his head against his brother and whispered: "Fighting Bear! He's outside at the window!"

A slight shiver raced down Jacques' spine, but after a long moment he put a reassuring hand on Dominic's head. His eyes remained perfectly calm as he spoke softly. "Have no fear, mon frère. He will do us no harm... his people would punish him severely. Now, go to your bed, and have good dreams."

Far into the night, Dominic was awakened. In the deep island stillness he heard the quiet, eerie sound of a drum, like the beating of a heart. But it wasn't coming from the distant Indian camp; it was very near, and it kept circling the house, on and on. Dominic knew it was Fighting Bear, attempting to weave some dark spell around the house of

Henri Bouton, around the soul that once was *Morning Star.*

Dominic crept silently to his father's bedroom door, where inside, Henri Bouton lay snoring. He had not been aroused by the strange sound of the drum, and he had not been disturbed earlier by the Indian's presence at the window. Perhaps it was just as Jacques had said. There was really nothing to fear. Yet, there it was—a phantom; something savage and secret and haunting.

# *Chapter 8*

*D*ominic barely recognized Silver Cloud, his cousin and childhood playmate.  He was three years older than Dominic, and he had grown tall since Dominic's last visit to their village, over three years ago, just before his mother died.

"My son will soon be a man," said Gray Wolf.  "He is a good hunter; he has listened carefully to all that I have taught him.  Soon he will be the one who will teach other young ones who follow."

Dominic gazed at tall, lean, muscular Silver Cloud with admiration when they went off together.  But his old playmate seemed to be drifting away from him, taking his rightful place in the established ways of Indian adult life and custom.  Dominic could understand that lifestyle, but he couldn't enter it; now, more than ever, he was puzzled by the emotions within that were tugging at his soul in opposite directions.  His loyalties were divided: he could not abandon his father's French heritage; nor could he be completely Indian.

"I suppose you will no longer want to play with me at so trifling a thing as bow-and-arrow target shooting," Dominic said.

Silver Cloud laid his arm across his cousin's shoulders.  "The bow-and-arrow is not trifling," said the Indian boy.  "It was the trusted weapon and good friend of the Old

Ones, and the Old Ones are very wise. It still fits the Indian hand as well as the leather glove of the white man. Come... let us play at target shooting right now."

It was a happy afternoon, far away from the island village where all the adults were conducting their trading. Dominic enjoyed running almost naked, covered only by a loin cloth, just like his older cousin. They played at target shooting, and then raced through the woods to the far side of the island where they swam from a sandy beach.

When darkness fell that night after a long, thrilling day and an evening feast, Dominic entertained his Indian relatives with his new flute as they danced around the campfires, drumming and singing the familiar traditional songs.

When the dancing ended and all the others had gone quietly to their tepees, Gray Wolf summoned Dominic to join him. They sat close, cross-legged for a few moments in the firelight. The crackling of the embers and the distant hoot of an owl were the only sounds as Gray Wolf retrieved something from his vest pocket. Ceremoniously he held out a small leather pouch tied tightly at the top with a long lanyard loop. The pouch was decorated with a painted symbol—a bird with outstretched wings. He spread the lanyard loop and slipped it over Dominic's head, placing it around his neck so that the pouch hung at the boy's chest. "Your grandfather, old and unable to come here now, instructed me to give you this, Little Otter."

"What is it?" asked Dominic.

"A medicine bag. It contains a few pebbles and grains of sand from your island...your homeland will now always be close to your heart, and it will protect you from the thunder in the night."

33

Tired, Dominic—Little Otter—slowly walked back to his house by the lagoon.  Although he didn't completely understand all that his uncle had just told him, he cherished the gift hanging around his neck.  It was a meaningful symbol of acceptance by his Indian family.

The island had fallen into near silence, with only the murmur of the river current gently washing the rocks along the bank and a soft summer breeze mischievously stirring the forest's branches.  He tumbled into his bed.

As he lay there before he fell asleep, he whispered to himself: "Yes, Silver Cloud is different now.  All the time, even when we're playing, he's thinking of something secret."

# Chapter 9

*O*n their last day together, Dominic was feeling a bit grumpy and out of sorts. He had not rested well because thoughts of things he did not completely understand kept him tossing and turning in a troubled sleep. That morning, neither he nor Silver Cloud was much in the mood for playing, but rather, they stole away to the far beach where they could be alone. They swam for a while, and then lay in silence on the sand watching the gulls swooping about. Finally, Dominic broke the silence. "You seem so far away," he said. "Don't you like me for a playmate anymore?"

Silver Cloud glanced at him in surprise. "Little Otter! Have you not noticed that the childhood of Silver Cloud is nearing the end? Have you forgotten that an Indian boy must perform his vigil before he becomes a man?"

Dominic just stared at him, puzzled.

Silver Cloud continued. "The time has come for me to go into the wilderness to fast and pray. When the moon is next round and bright in the sky, your cousin goes to receive a message from the Great Spirit—a message that will bring me good medicine, and will, perhaps, make me a great leader of my people." He stared deeply into Dominic's eyes as if to intensify the meaning of his words. "If all goes well, the Great Spirit will send me a sign in a dream, to guide me through all my days. This is a most important time for an Indian boy. That is why Silver Cloud seems so strange to you."

All of Dominic's selfish hurt vanished, even though Silver Cloud seemed even more distant now than he ever had. He was filled with awe and strangeness thinking about the hard task his cousin would soon undergo.

"The weather is hot," said Silver Cloud. "Let us go for another swim."

And for the rest of the long, happy afternoon the cousins seemed as once they were, two carefree boys together. Dominic glowed with pride when Silver Cloud praised his swimming. "It was I who taught you to swim under water. Remember? And now you are even more skillful. You well deserve the name of *Little Otter.*"

They laughed and whooped and splashed out of the water, raced each other across the sand, only to plunge into the water again, shouting cries of joy.

On the way back to the island village, they walked together slowly, lingering in the late afternoon sun. Silver Cloud spoke in low, serious tones. "In four days, Cousin, I go to make my vigil. Surely the Great Spirit will send me a vision, and he will give me a guardian spirit of my own. I have kept in my heart the words from the wise Old Ones in the council lodge; I have listened to my parents and have been obedient to them. I know that the Great Spirit gave us life and this earth on which we live. During the last few suns and moons I have tried to prepare myself to be worthy of a message from him."

They walked a little farther in silence. Silver Cloud's expression was bathed in concern. "This is what I have wanted to tell you today, before we say our farewells."

Dominic remained beyond speech. *To be so sure of your destiny, and to have your very own guiding spirit to*

36

*show you the way,* he thought, *being an* all-*Indian boy must be* magnifique.

"Pray for me, Little Otter, that my dream in the wilderness will bring a sign and that I will not return to my village like Fighting Bear."

Astonished, Dominic stared at his cousin. "Fighting Bear!" he said. "What—?"

"I was told that long ago Fighting Bear's quest for a vision was not successful. Instead, he returned to the village, near death, with wild fire in his eyes. He did not die because the evil spirits initiated him into the dark magic society."

"If he's so evil, why don't your people drive him away?"

"Because many believe he uses his dark magic, and they are afraid if he is exiled, he will cast a spell on the entire village and do great harm. So they don't want to anger him, and they allow him to stay."

Dominic recalled the night he saw Fighting Bear at the window. "So that's why..." He hesitated, and decided not to tell Silver Cloud about his strange experience. "Yes, Cousin, I will pray for your success."

# Chapter 10
## La Crosse; February 1878

"*W*elcome," said Captain Will Gordon as Frank McIntyre and his sister, the widow Mrs. Wood, entered the den. "I'm so glad you could make it." He rose from his chair, crossed the room and shook hands with his best friend. Then he took Mrs. Wood by the hand, caressed her cheek with a tender little kiss, and guided her to the sofa where she always liked to sit. The captain's daughter, Maria, greeted the two visitors from her place at the writing desk, and then came over to receive her customary hug from handsome Frank McIntyre. Since she was a little girl she had always admired Frank, and now that she was accepted as an adult, she was happy to always be included in the social conversations. Not that she had any romantic interest in Frank—he had always been more like an older brother. She sat beside Mrs. Wood and they immediately dove into conversation about the latest dress and hair styles while the two men engaged in discussion of riverboats over a couple of glasses of brandy. They were both experienced riverboat pilots on the Upper Mississippi.

"The McDonalds are building a new log rafter," Gordon said.

"Yes, I've heard the rumors," Frank replied.

"Oh, it's no rumor. They plan to have 'er on the river towing logs by the spring of 1880."

"And let me guess," Frank said. "You're gonna pilot this new boat."

"Better yet," Gordon said. "They're making me her captain."

"Well, congratulations, Will!" Frank raised his glass in an honorable salute.

"Thank you, my friend." Gordon then raised his glass. "And I sincerely hope that you will consider leaving the Davidson fleet and being my second pilot."

"Well, I don't know…"

"You don't have to answer right now, Frank. But do give it some thought, will you?"

Just then, Helen, the housekeeper entered the den and announced that she was ready to serve their supper in the dining room.

"Come, everyone," said the captain. "Let's see what savory delicacy Helen has prepared for us this evening."

They all filed into the dining room, following the enticing aroma. When they were seated, Helen began serving the roast duck, baked squash, fresh bread still warm from the oven, and all the garnishments to make the perfect meal.

"Would you still ask me to be your second pilot if I were to steal Helen from you?" asked Frank in a joking manner.

"Well," replied the captain. "I should be very lost without her. And I will definitely need her services when I adopt a son."

The statement took Frank and his sister by surprise, but they seemed delighted by the thought. "You're adopting a son?" Frank asked.

"Yes, I have been giving it much thought lately."

"And how do you plan to raise a son when you're on the river from March 'til November?"

"Why, Helen and Maria can care for him and teach him the art of being a gentleman while I'm away... until he's old enough to work aboard a boat. And then I intend to make him a pilot."

"A pilot!" Frank exclaimed.

"I think it's a wonderful idea," Mrs. Wood chimed in. "You know how much I adore my brother...why, I don't know what I'd do if anything ever happened to Frank. It would be such a nice addition to this household for Maria to have a little brother." She glanced across the table to Maria. "Don't you think so, my dear?"

Maria smiled. "Why, yes, it probably would be nice to have someone else here while Papa is away all summer."

Although Frank wasn't opposed to an adoption, he remained a little concerned. "And just where do you think you'll find this boy?"

Captain Gordon gazed into Frank's eyes. "Do you forget?" he said. "I have been on the board of guardians for the Mission School for several years, now. They have plenty of children who need homes."

"But the boys at the orphanage are nothing but a bunch of ruffians... probably illiterate... and certainly not gentlemen."

Gordon grinned. "A boy is a boy. He's made of flesh and blood. I don't care where he comes from. You can make of him whatever you want."

"Flesh and blood, yes," Frank replied. "But if he doesn't have the *right* blood, you can't make him a gentleman."

"Nonsense. It's just a matter of training and education."

"But Will... name one boy who came out of that school who amounted to any more than a common laborer... or a criminal."

"That's because no one ever took any interest in any of them when they were young... or gave them the guidance and opportunity to be anything better."

"I must say, Will... it'll be quite a challenge. Do you think you are up to that challenge?"

"Frank, you and your sister have been our best friends for years. I value your judgment and I respect your opinions. Yes, I think I'm up to the challenge of raising a son... to be a gentleman... and a riverboat pilot. I only ask you for your support."

## Chapter 11
## Summer: 1878

*C*aptain Gordon stood before the entryway at the Mission School.  Never before had he experienced such mixed emotions as he was feeling now.  There was the strong compassion; to give a young boy a good life; deliver him from this dismal existence of confinement; to offer him a family and a sense of belonging.  But Gordon also was quite aware of the background and origins of most of these children who, perhaps, may have experienced traumatic events that led to their being in this place, who had been abandoned by adults, and therefore had formed a high degree of distrust of adults.  Although he had been serving on a board of guardians for the school for several years, and had helped promote its support by the community, he had never become personally involved with its inhabitants, and he had no idea what to expect now.

He was determined, though, to take one of these boys into his home, nurture him to an adult, and transform him into an admirable legacy of which he could be proud. He was certain that with proper training and education, he could condition one of these boys into a gentleman. And after all, his good friend, Frank McIntyre had challenged him to the task.

"Good morning, Mr. Stanley," he greeted as the door opened.

"Good morning to you sir," Stanley replied. "Come to look around?"

"In a manner of speaking. Actually, I'm looking for a boy. Do you have any?"

"Boys, sir? The place swarms with them."

"Well then, show me some."

"Show you some, sir?"

"Yes. I want a boy."

"Certainly, sir. Come right this way. About what age, sir?"

"Not particular," said the captain. "Maybe about fourteen or fifteen."

Mr. Stanley rubbed his chin, as if deep in thought. "Strong young lad for chores around the dock?"

"Oh, no," replied Captain Gordon. "I want to adopt a boy."

"I see," Stanley said, wondering curiously if Captain Gordon was in his right mind. He led the captain through a passageway, and then across a sandy yard to a long, low building that served as the barracks for all the boys of the school, ranging in age from six to sixteen. All orphans, whose parents had become victims of the harshness presented by the frontier, they had somehow found their way here, and the Mission School was now their home until they were able to fend for themselves.

The hum of many voices rolled through the open windows. The boys had just finished their breakfast and were busy tidying up the barracks before they were dispatched to various chores. The noise ceased as if by magic, and 37 faces turned and every eye trained on the accompanying visitor as Headmaster Stanley opened the door.

The captain gazed upon the room, rows of bunks taking up most of the space with little room for anything else. He saw a crowd of heads and dull but curious expressions. All the boys seemed to have been poured from the same mold; all clad in the same gray trousers and faded pale blue shirts. They appeared to be adequately fed, and clean. But somehow, Gordon got the impression that they, perhaps, didn't *enjoy* the food, and were *too* clean, the clothes uncomfortable, and all were well on their way to becoming old men without having been allowed to stop and play, and to be boys.

"As you can see, Captain," Mr. Stanley said quietly, avoiding the boys hearing his words. "We are a bit crowded."

"Yes," agreed Gordon. "But I hope to free up one bed for you today."

Had the boys heard their conversation and known the purpose of the visit, there would have raised a tremendous yell that would have consisted of two words: *"Take me!"*

This was a good orphanage school—one which made the guardians proud; no tyranny or brutality, but there was endless discipline, and of course, the lack of the family-home-sweet-home factor. As hard as Stanley and his staff tried, they could not create that atmosphere for every child, and it must have been the absence of these elements that made the Mission boys look like 37 pale-faced little old men.

"Now, let me see," said the school master. "The matter will have to be put before the board in the usual manner, of course..."

"Usual manner?" Gordon said. "Do you forget that I am *on* that board, sir?"

"Yes. I mean, no, of course not, Captain." Mr. Stanley turned his head toward the boys. "Would you like to make your choice now, Captain?"

Gordon scanned the crowd of heads. "Yes... of course, you will make some suggestions?"

Stanley left the captain's side to stroll among the boys. He stopped occasionally, placed his hand on a shoulder, leaned and whispered something in a boy's ear. When he returned to Captain Gordon, seven boys followed and stood at attention before the master and his guest. Not one smiled, but rather displayed an expression as if he were about to be punished.

Stanley put his hand on the first boy's shoulder, a tall, very thin and pale boy who appeared as though he had been accidently whitewashed. "This is Cogan, a very fine lad; thirteen, and the best marks in his class." Then he moved on to the next boy in line. "This is Duffy, a very good boy..."

Stanley went down the line bragging about each of his selections. But none of them impressed Gordon, as they didn't seem to possess the spirit that he had come to expect in a boy. Once again he scanned the crowded bunk room until his eyes made contact with those of a boy way in the back. His wavy blonde hair glistened in a streak of sunlight coming through a window, and his blue eyes sparkled with... spirit!

"There," said Gordon. "Who is that boy?"

45

"Which one, sir?"

"The one in the back... the blonde-haired one standing all alone."

Stanley stared at the lone boy, and then with a low, troubled voice said to Gordon, "You mean... I can't recommend... sir... I don't think you want to consider him. He's not a very good boy."

Gordon's face beamed with pleasure, ignoring Stanley's warning. "Have him come here to me. I want to get a closer look and have a talk with him."

"But... sir... all of *these* boys are of the highest character..."

"*Now*, Mr. Stanley."

Reluctantly, Stanley turned and called out. "Jules Martin. Would you come here, please?"

The boy seemed pleasantly surprised that he would be chosen to join the group that he knew to be the smartest lads in the school. A worried smile squirmed on his face. He hadn't heard the proceedings from his far corner, and weaving his way to the front he wondered what kind of prank he was about to receive.

Stanley pulled Gordon aside and turned him so their backs were to the boys. "Captain Gordon, sir... that boy will not do," he said sternly.

"Why, how do you know that?" Gordon responded.

"Very bad boy, I'm sorry to say," the school master said. "Full of mischief that corrupts the other boys. Can't say a word in his favor... always being punished... and besides... he's younger than you want."

"How old is he?"

"About twelve, sir," Stanley said, and then added, "Yes, sir. Son of a miserable old tramp who died some years ago right here in our infirmary the night he brought the boy to us. The tramp had no identity, so we gave the boy his name."

When Gordon turned back toward the boys, Jules Martin had almost reached the front. The little fellow came full of eagerness and excitement after kicking a bully in the shin who had stuck out his foot trying to trip Jules.

Gordon frowned and gazed sternly at the boy, admirably taking in his handsome features, sparkling blue eyes, and wavy yellow hair that hung down on his forehead. Though it was thin, the boy's face didn't seem quite so pale as the others, nor was it depressed or mournful. His lips were rosy and smiling, and when they parted they revealed his pearly white teeth.

"The school master tells me that you are a bit of a rascal," Gordon said to the boy.

Jules wrinkled his forehead and glanced at Stanley before boldly casting his bright eyes on the Captain. "I d'know," he said, puzzled.

"You don't know, *SIR!*" Stanley said, correcting the boy's lack of respect.

"I'm sorry, sir... you see? I don't mean to, but I'm always findin' trouble..."

"What's your name, lad?"

"Jules Martin."

*"SIR!"* spouted the school master.

"Jules Martin, SIR," the boy said quickly, correcting his error.

"What a name!" said Gordon.

"Yes, ain't it, though? I hate it, sir."

"You do?"

"Yes, sir. All the other boys make fun of it. They call

47

me Julie most of the time, just because..."

Laughter and snickering interrupted him.

"That will do, Mr. Martin," Stanley said. "Don't ramble so."

"Please, sir. He asked me," the boy said in protest. There was a sincere tone in his voice that sat well with Captain Gordon.

"With all due respect, Mr. Stanley," Gordon said. "Please let me talk to the boy."

"Certainly, sir. But he has a very bad record." Stanley was still trying to convince the captain that he had made a wrong choice.

"But he seems truthful. I'll be the judge of his record, Mr. Stanley," Gordon said with a forbidding tone. Then he turned back to the boy and grinned. "Would you like to leave this place?"

The boy's eyes squinted questioningly. He took a step forward, and Stanley moved in as if to force a retreat, but Gordon blocked him with a stiff arm. The boy looked on, intensity multiplying, knowing that the captain was defending him.

"Well?" said Gordon. "Do you want to come and live at my place?"

The boy's face smoothed into a pleasant little smile. Bright light danced in his eyes, and full of confidence he said eagerly, "Yes." He held out his hand.

"And leave all your schoolmates?" Gordon said, taking the boy's hand in his.

Jules' bright face clouded. He turned to gaze at all the scowls of jealousy. Then he looked back to Gordon and nodded.

"He'll be glad to go," Stanley said. "Most ungrateful

boy."

The boy swung sharply around toward Mr. Stanley. Now the sparkles in his eyes were tears. "I didn't want to be bad, sir," he sputtered. "I did try, and... and..." He could say no more, and at last, in shame and agony he covered his face with his hands and dropped to his knees on the puncheon floor, sobbing hysterically.

"Jules! Stand up!" the school master ordered sternly.

"Let him be, Mr. Stanley," Gordon said. He drew in a deep breath and remained silent for a long moment, while the other boys stared in wonder, and he and Stanley exchanged glances.

"Strange boy," said Stanley.

Then Gordon knelt down slowly and caressed the boy's shoulder with a gentle hand. Jules flinched at first, but as soon as he realized who was touching him, he quickly clutched Gordon's hand and rose to his feet. The gaze from Gordon's eyes had a strange influence on him, and he couldn't look away.

"I think you'll come with me now?" Gordon said.

"Yes... but... may I?" Jules' watery eyes pleaded with Mr. Stanley.

Stanley nodded approval to the boy. "Yes, of course, if you wish." Then he turned to Gordon. "I shall have to bring your proposal before the board."

"That is to say, before me and my colleagues," Gordon said smiling. "Well, as one of the Guardians of this school, I think I may venture to take the boy now, and the formal business can be settled later."

"Yes, of course, sir. And I venture to think that it will not be necessary to continue with the formalities."

"And why not, Stanley?"

"Because," the school master said with a peculiar grin. "You will bring him back within a week."

"I will not be bringing him back, Stanley. I have made my decision, and I am certain it is the right one," Gordon said. He laid his hand on the boy's golden head.

"Very well, but if you want to take him now, his clothes must be…"

"He will not be needing his clothes or anything more from the Mission. I will see to that."

"Very well, sir. I hope he will take your kindness to heart." Mr. Stanley leaned closer to the boy. "Did you hear, Jules? Try to be good for Captain Gordon. He seems to like you."

"Yes, yes, yes, Mr. Stanley," Gordon cut him off short. "He will be just fine. Now my little man… are you ready to go?"

"Yes, sir, but…"

"What is it?" Gordon asked.

"May I go say good-bye to my friends and Mother Champlain?"

Captain Gordon gave a curious glance to Stanley. "Mother Champlain?"

"Nurse, sir. The woman who cared for him when he was just a little thing… right after the old tramp died."

"Ah, well certainly. Run along, then, and say your good-byes."

The boy looked up into his eyes with question.

"No," Gordon said, sensing the boy's sudden fear. "I will not run away without you. I will be waiting for you at the gate."

The boy darted away to the main hall and disappeared into a doorway.

While the boy was seeking the old woman, Stanley led the way to the front gate. "He has no friends, you know," he said to Gordon. "And I must warn you of his character."

"No offense, Stanley," Gordon interrupted. "But I think I would like to discover his true character on my own."

Just then Jules and an elderly woman met them at the gate.

"You are a fortunate man," she said. "He is such an affectionate boy." Jules was clinging to her apron. "Good-bye and good luck," she said, and leaned down to kiss the boy in a motherly fashion.

He hugged her affectionately, as if she were the only being he thought he could ever love.

"God bless you, my dear boy," Mrs. Champlain whispered.

As Captain Gordon and Jules passed through the gate and down the walkway toward his waiting carriage, Mrs. Champlain commented, "Very nice man."

"Yes," replied Stanley. "But he'll bring the rascal back."

The captain didn't hear. His attention was focused on Jules who clung tightly to his hand, fighting hard to hold back the tears.

Gordon couldn't help but notice. He gently squeezed the boy's hand.

# Chapter 12

*O*n the way to Captain Gordon's house, Jules' heart swelled with sorrow, having to part from Mrs. Champlain, the only person who had been at all kind to him; his recollection of the rough tramp had become quite faint, and he certainly wouldn't miss many of the other boys at the Mission School, who had generally made him their object of teasing and torment. Now it was the captain who offered kindness, but there hadn't been an opportunity, yet, for Jules to evaluate all this that was happening so quickly.

Helen, the captain's housekeeper, met them at the door with an expression of surprise. Captain Gordon had instructed her earlier to prepare an upstairs bedroom, but she wasn't expecting such a young guest.

"Helen, I would like you to meet Jules Martin," Captain Gordon said. He put his arm across the boy's shoulders and pulled him close. "He will be my adopted son. I trust that you have his room ready?"

Helen's eyes opened wide as if shocked by some disturbing news, and her expression turned to a worried one. She recognized the clothing of the Mission School, and she wasn't entirely sure that she was prepared to have a youngster in the house again, much less, an unrefined imp from the orphanage. Helen had been the housekeeper since Mrs. Gordon's passing, and she had cared for Maria, Mr. Gordon's daughter. But that was different—Maria was a girl.

*And this was a boy! How could she tolerate a boy?*

Jules seemed amused by Helen's facial antics, and he smiled. "Pleased to meet you, Miss Helen," he said. The housekeeper didn't immediately impress him as being the loving, caring, warm person that Mrs. Champlain had been, but he thought he should be polite to her, anyway.

Helen gave a courteous little bow. "If you will excuse me, sir, I will go to finish getting his room ready."

"Very well," said Gordon. "Where's Maria?"

"I believe she's in the study," the maid replied.

"Good. Then that's where we'll be, introducing Maria to her new little brother."

After Helen had disappeared up the staircase, Jules turned to Captain Gordon. "She doesn't like me much, do she?"

"Oh, give her time, my boy. Give her time. Helen's a very good woman." He guided the boy down the hall to an open doorway that led into a very comfortable-looking den, the walls lined with bookshelves and paintings, the floor covered with carpet, a luxurious sofa and easy chairs, and in one corner flanked by draped windows on either side was a writing desk where sat beautiful Maria. She looked up from the letter she was writing and gazed wonderingly at the boy standing directly in front of her father. "Hello, Papa," she said after turning her quizzical stare to a pleasant smile. "You're back."

"Yes, my dear. Maria, this is Jules Martin. Shake hands with him and make him feel at home."

The captain's sweet, lady-like daughter held out her hand to the boy, who was gazing all around the room with curious delight until his eyes fell upon an elegantly framed, admirably crafted water color portrait of the captain hanging on the wall. It was the work of Maria.

Jules burst into a hearty laugh, ran to Maria and took her hand.  He pointed with his left hand to the portrait. "Look at that... it's the cap'n's picture.  Ain't it like him, though?"

Maria looked troubled with the boy's roughness, even though he had just paid a compliment to her artistic skill.

A long moment of painful silence was broken by Jules pumping Maria's hand up and down.  "How do you do, Miss Maria?" he said solemnly.

A warm smile rippled over Maria's face.  The boy's expression brightened, and he, too, smiled in such a way that made him look quite handsome and attractive, despite his forlorn attire.  "Oh, but ain't you pretty?  Prettier than any gal I ever seen before."

"Ah, yes," the captain interrupted.  "Now, Jules... Mr. Stanley, your school master said that you were anything but a good boy."

"Yeah, everybody knows that I'm the worst bad boy in the whole school."

Maria grimaced.

"Oh, you are, are you," Gordon said.

"Yeah.  Mr. Stanley told everybody I am."

"But you will start being a good boy from now on?"

"All right, sir."

"And behave yourself like a little gentleman?"

"But... am I gonna stay here?"

"Yes."

"And I ain't goin' back to the school for supper and breakfuss?"

"No, you will eat here with us."

"But will I have to go back and sleep in the dormitory with the other boys?"

"No, you will sleep in your room upstairs."

"Here?  In this beautiful house?  With you?  And this nice lady?"

"Yes, of course."

The boy was almost in tears. "Yyyaahooooooo!" he cried in a screeching voice, and then with all the grace of a practiced circus performer he went hands over feet cartwheels in a circle completely around the room, coming to rest perfectly in front of Captain Gordon.

"Here, now!  There will be no more of that in this house!" the captain scolded, half angry and half amused.

The boy stood there with such innocent pride.  After a few moments of feeling a little annoyed with the boy's behavior, Maria sat back in her chair and laughed, as much at her father's puzzled look as at the boy.

When he saw that Maria seemed amused, he turned to her and said, "That's nothing.  Watch this!"  And before they could protest against any more acrobatic tricks, Gordon and Maria watched as the boy quickly stepped in front of the fireplace, ducked down with his hands planted firmly on the carpet, and then kicked his heels in the air.

"Get down, my boy!  Get down!" begged the captain. "No, I mean... get up!"

"But I'm not done," said Jules.  He tipped his legs backward for balance as he walked on his hands in a small circle, lowered his feet to the floor and sprang up as if he had just done a backward flip, directly facing Mr. Gordon. His handsome young face beamed with proud delight.

Gordon caught hold of the boy's strong arms and held him firmly.  "Confound you, boy.  You certainly are full of the Dickens."

Maria tried to look serious.  She held her handkerchief

to hide her smiling face, but her eyes twinkled with joy. Her father's plan to raise a gentleman from an orphanage ruffian was certainly off on a rocky start.

"Jules... are you hungry?" she said, hoping to get his mind off any more acrobatic demonstrations.

The boy shook himself loose from the captain and ran to Maria. "Is it dinnertime already?"

"No, but you've had a very busy morning, and perhaps you would like a piece of cake."

Jules stared at Maria, and then at the captain, puzzled. "Is it somebody's birthday?"

"No," Maria said.

"Y' mean... y' have cake here... even when it's *not* somebody's birthday?"

"Oh, yes, my boy," Mr. Gordon replied. "And lots of other good things, too. You'll see."

Maria crossed the room to the hall, summoned Helen, and requested her to bring the cake she had baked that morning, a knife, plate, and a glass of milk. Helen soon returned with a tray that she placed on a table, staring at the boy with anything but favorable eyes.

"You're having milk?" said the boy to Maria.

"Oh, no... it's for you."

"For me?"

"Yes," Maria said. Then she cut a generous wedge of cake, put it on the plate, and slid it and the milk toward Jules. She glanced at her father who sat quietly, brow furrowed, thinking out his plans.

Jules watched her with sparkling eyes, and it pleased Maria the way he examined her, for on the outside he was displaying, at that moment, his school discipline, but on the inside she sensed a little savage, eager and full of curiosity.

"Was that your sister who brought the cake?" Jules asked.

"No, Helen is our servant. She's been our housekeeper since Mama fell ill and passed away many years ago, when I was just a little girl."

"Oh," Jules said. "Kinda like Mother Champlain. She took care of me for as long as I can remember, but they say she's not really my mother." He looked at the piece of cake Maria had given him. "Would y' cut this again? In three? I'd like ever so much to share it with Mother Champlain and Jimmy."

"Who's Jimmy?" Maria asked.

"He's m' best pal at th' school... been sick in bed with th' measles. But he's getting better now, and I know he'd like some cake, too."

"You shall have more cake to send to Mrs. Champlain and Jimmy if you wish. That whole piece is for you. Now, you sit here quietly and eat your cake."

Maria felt her eyes getting a little moist. The boy's genuine unselfish, generous spirit caressed her soul, and she looked at him with a renewed interest. She smiled and laid her hand on his shoulder.

Jules put his hand on hers, like a cat lays a paw in a gesture of affection. As the strange little fellow munched on the cake she didn't take her hand away until her father said sharply, "Maria, come here."

The boy stared, but he went on eating as Maria crossed the room to where Captain Gordon sat.

"Yes, Papa?"

"About this boy..." the captain said.

Maria's heart sank. She didn't know why, but she had suddenly felt a warm closeness to the boy. If she had been asked, she could not have explained her rising compassion for this odd little guy who she feared, now, that her father was about to reject. "You want to raise a boy," she said to her father in a tone that Jules was unable to hear. "But you are taking him back to the school and will select another."

Captain Gordon gazed at his daughter with a questioning expression. "Why would I want to do that?"

"I thought..." Maria hesitated. "I thought you wanted a gentleman son, polished and cultured."

"Oh, nonsense! So he's a little wild and rough; he's a boy—a high-spirited boy, that's all. He's got the right stuff in him."

"But he is so very rough," Maria smiled.

"A *little* rough, maybe," said the captain. "But we can make him a gentleman, and that's why I ask you now to help me with the poor orphan. He seems to like you."

"So... he's an orphan?"

"Yes, the son of some miserable old tramp who just wandered in with the boy and died there in the infirmary."

"Oh, how dreadful. And sad." Maria glanced at the boy. He smiled in a way that made his face light up.

"You see, my dear?" the captain said. "Just look at him. Behind those rough edges is a handsome, charming boy... a gentleman he shall be, with our help, of course."

"Very well, Papa," said Maria. "I will help you all I can."

"Thank you, my dear," the captain said warmly. "I know that someday you will be proud of your efforts, and so shall I. Now, then, where to begin?"

# Chapter 13
## The Transformation Begins

*N*oticing the pleased looks on their faces, Jules leaped up from his stool as if preparing to perform another gymnastic feat.

"NO!  Sit down!" shouted the captain, and the boy dropped meekly back onto his seat.

"There," said the captain.  "You see, Maria?  We've already achieved obedience.  Now... for the next order of business, the boy needs some good clothes."

Jules spoke up.  "Oh, that won't be necessary, sir," he said eagerly.  "I have more of these in my trunk at the dormitory."

"Nonsense.  You will not be wearing poor orphan child's clothing anymore.  Mr. Markos, the haberdasher in town, will come to measure you for all new ones."  Then he turned to Maria.  "See what you can do to trim his hair, will you?"  He stared at the boy's golden locks that were cut uneven and ragged.  "I do believe the barber at the school should be flogged."

Mr. Gordon paced across the room and back again, pulled out his pocket watch and glanced at the time.  "I have some business down at the boatyard, and I will stop by the haberdasher's.  But before I go, there's one more thing."  He sat down in his easy chair.  "Come here, my boy."

Jules jumped to his feet and went to the captain with

bold strides. He stood before Gordon with expectant eyes.

"You told me back at the school that you don't like your name."

"No, sir, I don't."

"Well, then, we'll do away with that right now. What name *do* you like?"

The boy shrugged his shoulders and threw his hands out to the side. His eyes rolled around, searching the ceiling and the walls, and then finally came back to the captain with uncertainty. "I d'know, sir... Jack?"

"No, no, no. Let's see," Mr. Gordon said, rubbing his chin. "How do you like Charles? That's a good gentleman's name."

The boy's lips pursed; his eyes squinted in deep thought. After a long moment his white teeth beamed a broad smile. "Okay," he replied. "Charles Martin sounds good."

"But your official name," said the captain, "will be Charles Martin Gordon from now on. You are to be my son, so it's only fitting and proper that you should have the name as well."

The boy was truly happy with all that had transpired, so far, and he was about to utter his thank you, but he stopped short to first swipe his nose with the cuff of his shirt sleeve.

Captain Gordon immediately turned to Maria. "Tell Helen to monogram a dozen handkerchiefs with CMG for the boy."

Maria nodded.

The boy grinned. "A dozen handkerchiefs all for me?"

"Yes," said the captain. "And don't let me catch you wiping your nose on your sleeve again, okay?"

Charles nodded. He realized that he had been on the receiving end of generosity much to his advantage, and he was quite certain that it all would come at a price. To show the captain that he was willing to accept responsibilities in return, before he was asked, he offered, "What chores will I be doing? Fetch water from the well? Clean the stables? Till the garden? Fill the coal buckets?"

Mr. Gordon laughed. "Aren't you the eager one? You need not worry about any of that for now. Maria will take charge of you for the time being and get you settled in."

"But I will go to my classes at the school?"

"My boy, Charles... I want you to forget that school and everything about it."

"Forget it?" Charles replied with his forehead puckered up.

"In time, Charles, we will send you to a good school. But for now, Maria will teach you all you need to know," Gordon said, and then he got up out of his chair and strolled to the door. He turned to Maria. "Tell Helen that I will be back about six for supper. And Mr. Markos will be by sometime this afternoon to measure Charles for his new clothes, so be watching for him."

"Yes, Papa," Maria said. "I'll take good care of Charles Martin for you till you get back."

After the captain was gone, Charles sat on a hassock. A troubled expression came on his face, and Maria knelt down before him.

"What's the matter?" she asked. "You look worried."

Charles gazed into her eyes for a long moment. "I... I... I never had a father... that I remember, anyway. I... I never had nobody... 'cept Mother Champlain, and she wasn't really my mum."

Maria saw tears beginning to form in his eyes, and she was sure they were tears of joy. She stretched out her arms to him, inviting him to be hugged. He leaned forward, laid his cheek on her shoulder, and soaked up the embrace for at least a minute. Then he pushed himself back onto the hassock and wiped away the tears with the back of his hand.

With a slight crackle still in his voice he said, "But what do I call him?"

Maria smiled. "Oh, I guess you should call him *Father,* or *Papa*, like I do, or you can call him *Sir*... he likes that."

"And you are his daughter. What should I call you?"

"Well, since I am going to be your sister, you should just call me Maria."

He absorbed all that very quickly. "Maria?"

"Yes."

"If I'm not going back to th' school, I won't ever get to see th' boys... or Mother Champlain."

"I'm sure you will make lots of new friends, and perhaps Papa will allow Mrs. Champlain to come visit you here sometime."

"Oh! That would be grand!" Charles grinned. "Could you save her a bit of that cake for when she comes?"

Maria laughed. "I'll have Helen bake another cake... just for Mrs. Champlain." She couldn't help but feel pleased with the boy's concern of others.

In less than an hour, Mr. Markos, the haberdasher arrived at the front door. Helen escorted him to the den where Maria was teaching Charles a few points of protocol and etiquette for the Gordon home, as she knew that her father would expect good manners from Charles very soon.

Mr. Markos gave a little bow to the young lady, and then glanced to the center of the room where the boy still sat obediently on the hassock. "Ah... this must be Charles," he said with a reserved grin, recognizing the orphanage attire. "Mr. Gordon said he was a handsome lad in need of some new clothes." He winked at the boy. "I see he was quite right on both accounts."

Mr. Markos was dressed in a dapper brown suit, white shirt with collar and necktie that matched the suit. His shoes were shined to mirrors, and Charles found him quite pleasant. Even with Charles standing on the hassock, Mr. Markos stood at least a head taller than him, so the tailor still had to lean and stoop to get all the measurements. Charles giggled in amusement as the tailor's hands tickled certain spots. This was a new experience for the boy; he'd never been fussed over like this before... ever. Whenever he had gotten clothes at the school, they were usually well worn hand-me-downs that were always too big, so that he would grow into them by the end of the year when the same process would happen again.

"Sit down, now, and take off your boots so I can measure your feet for some new shoes," Mr. Markos said to Charles.

"New shoes, too!" Charles said.

"Why, yes. Mr. Gordon told me to fit you with anything you need and want. And you certainly could use a new pair of boots."

When Mr. Markos was finished taking the measurements he told Maria the new wardrobe would be ready in a week.

"Oh dear," cried Maria. "A week! And what is the boy to wear until then? He certainly can't go like this!" She nodded to the boy's shabby gray trousers and faded blue shirt, a hole worn in one elbow, making sure the tailor understood her feeling of urgency.

"Well," replied Mr. Markos. "Ready-made, ma'am? I have plenty of new and fashionable garments that would fit the boy perfectly. I could send them over to him yet this afternoon."

"Yes, by all means," said Maria. "Shirts, trousers, jacket, stockings, undergarments... everything... so he will have nice clothes until next week."

"Very well, ma'am. A nice selection will be here this afternoon."

Helen escorted Mr. Markos to the front door.

"A charming little fellow," he said to the housekeeper, and now even Helen was beginning to soften just a bit.

Back in the den, Charles' bright blue eyes sparkled as he thought about all the new clothes he would soon have, and he commenced a triumphant freestyle dance of spins, shuffles, kicks and flips that would have put an opera house stage performer to shame. Maria caught him by his hand and stopped him. "Okay, Charles Martin! That is quite enough. No more of that in here. Papa wouldn't approve."

"But it was because I was so happy! That's all."

"I understand," said Maria. "But Papa wants you to become a gentleman, and you must start to understand that you will no longer be without."

"Without what?" the boy said curiously.

"Anything a boy... a young gentleman... wants or needs. And if you're a good boy, I know Papa will make sure you have everything you'll need."

"And if I'm not a good boy? Will I get th' switch?"

Maria's expression turned somber. Was this his story of his past at the school? "I don't know. I hope that won't ever be necessary. You just have to learn to be a young gentleman."

"Gentleman? Y' means one of them that wears fancy black suits and turn-down collars and tall hats... and struts down th' street with a silver-handled walkin' stick?"

"Well, maybe not to that degree, yet, but Papa will expect you to have good manners and dress and act nicely... not like some primitive imp."

"Okay, Maria," said Charles. "I'll try real hard."

That reply was all Maria could expect.

After a lunch of ham sandwiches and a rhubarb tart with custard that Helen served them in the dining room, Maria thought there would be enough time to trim Charles' hair, and perhaps a bath. She requested Helen to prepare the bath while she and Charles went to her upstairs dressing room. She sat him in a chair and draped a sheet around him. As she combed and snipped away at his wavy blonde hair, she could only hope that her efforts—to make this boy one of which her father could be proud—would not be in vain. Now that he had won her affection, it would be an unbearably painful day when the boy was sent back to the Mission School, if he didn't measure up to her father's expectations, and somehow, she feared that was still a possibility.

"What does he do?" the boy asked.

"What do you mean?" Maria returned.

"Your *Papa.* He seems very nice. And he must be rich, to have such a fine house, and to buy me all those wonderful new clothes."

"Well, yes, Papa is quite well-to-do. He's a riverboat pilot... and Mississippi River pilots are some of the best-paid professionals these days."

"Oh, that's grand! D'ya think he'd take me for a ride on his boat someday?"

"I'm sure he will, in due time, Charles. I'd bet that he has plans for your future. But you best not pester him about that just yet."

When she was through cutting, she held up her vanity mirror so he might see what she had done. Not accustomed to often seeing his own image, the reflection in the mirror pleased him.

Just then, Helen knocked at the open door. She held two bundles wrapped in brown paper and tied with string. "These were delivered from Mr. Markos just a few minutes ago," she said, and then she eyed the youngster with his perfectly fashioned new haircut.

He threw back the sheet from around his shoulders and smiled. "Do you like it, Miss Helen?" he said.

Helen felt her reluctance to having a young boy in the house melting away. His charm was busy working its magic on her, too, but she resisted the urge to run into the room and kiss his rosy cheeks. She smiled. "Maria did a very nice job on your haircut... very handsome, indeed." Then Helen turned to leave, but quickly returned. "Maria," she added, "the bath is ready for Master Charles in his room."

"Thank you, Helen," Maria replied, and Helen carried the packages to Charles' room and disappeared down the stairs.

Maria guided the boy down the hallway to another bedroom. She ushered him inside, where Helen had left the new clothing on the bed, and where a bathtub filled with warm water rested in the middle of the room.

Charles gazed around the nicely decorated room. Royal blue drapes half covered a large window; a full-length mirror hung on one wall; on another wall was a painting of mountains and a river; a bird's-eye maple gentleman's dresser stood beside a matching East Lake double bed, a thick soft mattress covered with a plush royal blue quilt. Charles had never seen anything quite like it before. "What room is this?" he questioned.

"Your bedroom," Maria said.

"This is *my* room?"

"Yes," Maria replied. "All yours."

"Y' mean… this is where I'll sleep? All th' time?"

"Yes, Charles. This will always be *your* room. And Helen has prepared a nice warm bath for you. When was the last time you had a bath?"

"Last Saturday," Charles said. "Saturday is always my bath day at the sch…" He hesitated.

"What's wrong?" Maria asked.

"Mr…. I mean… Sir… I mean, *Father*… said I should forget everything about th' old school."

Maria smiled an understanding smile. "That's okay. Now you can have your bath in the privacy of your own room anytime you wish."

"Y' mean… right now?"

"Sure." Maria turned to examine the wrapped bundles on the bed. "Then we can see the new clothes Mr. Markos sent you, and you can try them on." When Maria looked his way again, Charles had disrobed completely, his old Mission clothes in a heap on the floor. The sight of him naked took her breath away. Now she understood why he could perform all those difficult acrobatic stunts so easily—he was quite muscular and well developed for his age. But there was something else that drew her attention: his reflection in the mirror behind him revealed several red scars, like those made by a whip, on his back and buttocks. She turned away quickly.

"What's wrong, Maria?"

"It's… it's not proper for me to see you… like that."

"Why?"

"Because I'm a lady, and you're a bo… a gentleman."

"So what? Mother Champlain saw me like this many times. She even put ointment on the sores after I got wh…" Charles stopped and thought for a moment. "There I go again… rememberin' th' old school." He climbed into the tub and submersed himself up to his neck into the warm, soothing water. "You can look again. I'm under the water now."

Maria reluctantly turned toward the bathing boy. "The soap is on that little table behind the tub, and your towel is on the bed. I'll be in my room down the hall. Call for me when you're done and I'll help you with your new clothes."

# Chapter 14

*C*aptain Gordon returned home just before six o'clock.

Helen took his coat and hat to be hung in the hall closet under the staircase. "Supper will be on the dining room table in about twenty minutes," she told him. "And I have your coffee waiting for you in the den."

The captain was glad he had Helen; she always satisfied him with the simplest pleasures... like coffee waiting in the den.

"And where are Maria and Charles?" he asked.

Helen grinned. "Oh, they will be down in time for supper, I'm sure."

"Did Mr. Markos come by to measure the boy?"

"Sure, he did."

"Good. Then I trust we will see the boy clad in descent clothes in a few days."

Helen just grinned some more, knowing the surprised look on Mr. Gordon's face would soon be a priceless treasure. She returned to the kitchen while Gordon went to the den to enjoy his evening coffee before supper.

He was reading the newspaper when Helen announced that supper was ready. Gordon followed her into the dining room where he sat down at the head of the table. He seemed a little irritated that the others were not already there. He should not have to wait for them.

"Oh, be patient, for once," Helen said. "Maria has been busy tutoring your little *gentleman* all afternoon. I think I hear them coming down the stairs now."

In all her radiant beauty Maria entered the room dressed in a lovely pale blue evening gown, appropriate for a formal dinner. She stepped aside to reveal behind her an attractively dressed, handsome young man standing in the doorway. His golden hair, trimmed and perfectly combed, glistened in the lamp light; his dark blue suit fit him precisely over a crisp white shirt with turn-down collar and black batwing tie; his boots shined like a newly-minted Double Eagle.

At first glance, Captain Gordon wondered what stranger his daughter had invited to supper, and then the astonishment overcame him as he realized the stranger was his newly-adopted son, Charles Martin. He looked the boy over from head to toe. The new clothes seemed to define the boy's well-cut features in a different air. The captain was speechless.

Charles offered Maria his arm and escorted her to her chair on her father's right, held the chair for her as she sat. Then he quietly crossed behind the captain, pulled out his chair and sat down, a worried half-smile dimpling his cheeks as he glanced at Maria and then at the captain, and then looked down into the tablecloth.

The captain watched, still unable to make a sound.

"Papa!" cried Maria. "Say something. Anything. Don't you approve?"

Helen stood by, grinning. She hadn't seen anything this amusing in that house for years.

"Yes, yes, my dear," the captain finally spurted out as he continued to stare at the boy. "I just don't know what to say."

That remark was quite unexpected, as the captain

usually voiced freely his opinions and comments in any situation. "Well, you could start by telling Charles that he looks nice… that his new clothes are very attractive."

Gordon gave his daughter and indignant stare. Then he turned to Charles. "Are you the same raggedy little boy I left here this morning?" he asked with a warm smile.

"Y-yes, sir, I-I believe so, sir," said Charles nervously.

"Well, it looks as though my daughter has performed some sort of miracle in the span of a few short hours." He turned back to Maria. "But where did these clothes come from. Mr. Markos said he'd be at least a week getting them finished."

"Ready-made, Papa. Mr. Markos had these in his store. Aren't they nice? He sent over enough so Charles would have something to wear until next week."

"Smart," the captain said. "That Markos has a good head on his shoulders. Now, Helen, I believe we're ready to eat."

All the fine China plates, silver, and sparkling glassware captured Charles' attention; for the moment he forgot his hunger until Helen brought in a platter with a dome-shaped cover, and soon the aroma of roasted beef filled the room. She carefully set the platter on the table next to the captain, removed the cover, and eyed Charles with uncertain admiration; she still wasn't completely comfortable with the idea of a boy in the house, especially a little heathen dressed in angel's clothing.

Charles grabbed his knife and fork in fisted hands and tapped their handles on the table at either side of his plate with eager anticipation.

"Put those down, Charles, and be patient," said the captain.

The boy quickly obeyed; his hands dropped to his sides and he watched with big eyes as Mr. Gordon began slicing the roast.

"Would you like a piece of meat now, my dear?" he said to Maria.

She held her plate close to the platter so her father could easily fork a dainty slice of beef onto it. Then he turned to Charles. "How about you, my boy? Would you like some meat now?"

"Oh yes, sir. A big piece... please." His eyes beamed.

The captain frowned just a little, and then gave the boy a generous chunk of meat on his plate.

"We don't get meat like this at th' school... only in stew... if ever," Charles said, and he started cutting and devouring the succulent meat at a furious pace.

"Easy does it!" said the captain. "And what did I say about you speaking of the old school?"

Charles stopped chewing abruptly, glanced at Maria, and then at Gordon. "I'm used to eating fast, 'cuz th' bell will ring and we have to make room at th' table for th' next..." He hesitated a long moment in thought. "Oh... th' bell won't ring here, will it?"

"No, my boy," the captain said sternly. "There are no bells here to make you hurry through your supper. Now, you don't have bread or vegetables yet. And try to behave like Maria and me at the table..."

"Papa," Maria intervened. "Don't be so hard on the boy all at once, or he can't enjoy his supper."

Gordon gazed at his daughter, saying nothing, but his eyes said, *"I see you have become quite fond of the boy."*

Charles accepted a boiled potato and a slice of bread on his plate only because he thought he *had* to, and then went back to the savory beef that was such a treat to him, this time at a painfully slow pace.

Except for the distinct ticking of the clock, for the next few minutes there were no sounds in the dining room but knives and forks scraping on the plates while all three continued their meal. Then the captain broke the silence. "So, tell me, son," he said in a non-threatening tone. "How do you like your new clothes?"

Charles swallowed hard while he thought briefly about his answer. For quite obvious reasons, he was not accustomed to crisp new clothing. He thought the skin might be rubbed off his legs, and one boot pinched just a little, and the starched and buttoned collar might saw his head off. But he didn't dare complain of any of that for fear that something dreadful might result. "Oh, I like 'em just fine," he said. "I'm sure I'll get used to 'em if I may keep 'em."

"Well, of course you may keep them," the captain replied. "But you must promise to take care of them, like a good boy."

"Oh, yes, sir. I will try to be a very good boy." Charles started to reach for the captain's hand, a gesture that he intended to be one of warm appreciation and affection, but his sudden movement knocked a glass off the table. His instant reaction took him off his chair to retrieve it, but when he stooped down, he saw the glass was broken.

"Oh dear!" the captain exclaimed sharply.

The boy misinterpreted Gordon's remark as anger and in one swift movement he was cowered on the floor in a corner with his knees to his chest, sobbing. "I couldn't help it, sir. Don't beat me this time, sir. I promise it won't happen again."

He wanted to dash out of the room or leap out a window, but Helen was there kneeling beside him, preventing him from bolting away. "Bless your soul, you poor child," she said in a pitiful tone. She looked defiantly at the captain, knowing that he respected her position on maintaining good order in the household. "There shall be no beating of a child in this house," she added. Charles' cry for mercy had secured his future with the housekeeper.

Maria was there by him then, too, tears in her eyes. "It was an accident, that's all," she said to the boy softly as she read the agony in his spirit. She urged him to his feet and guided him to his chair at the table, remaining by his side as he clung tightly to her hand.

"I wasn't going to beat you." Gordon reached toward the boy, intending to gently stroke his hair, but Charles flinched away, like a frightened animal anticipating punishment.

"I thought you looked like you was," the boy said, still sobbing. "You sounded angry."

"Perhaps I looked a little cross because you were clumsy and broke the glass," Gordon said. "But I realize, now, that it really was an accident." Then he looked at Maria. "Come sit down again, my dear. Let's finish our supper."

She gently kissed the boy's blond head and returned to her seat.

"Charles," the captain said. "I don't want you to be afraid of me. You and I should become the best of friends... you have my word."

Charles wiped away his tears with a napkin, tried to smile, and then completed the gesture he had intended before the glass fell. He carefully laid his small hand on the captain's for just a moment, and he said not a word.

The meal was resumed, but Charles' appetite was gone. He even had difficulty eating just a little of the baked apple with cinnamon and cream. This most recent incident, along with the entire day's events, lay heavy on his mind. "Would it be all right if I went up to th' room where Maria said I will sleep?" he asked. "I am so very tired."

The captain called Helen into the dining room. "Will you please see Master Charles to his room and help him get ready for bed?"

If someone had told Helen that morning that she would be acting toward the boy as she was now, she would have laughed in utter denial. But in the course of just one day, the boy's charming innocence had captured her adoration. She graciously bowed to the captain and then offered her hand to the boy. "Come along, lad," she said. "You've had a long hard day. Let's get you tucked in."

When he was in his nightshirt and Helen had him settled into the big, comfortable bed, Charles looked up into her eyes. "Will he send me back to the Mission School?" he whispered hoarsely.

Helen smiled and hesitated while she brushed back his golden hair. "Not if *I* have anything to say about it, *Charlie Martin.*"

He giggled. "You called me Charlie. I like that."

Helen just smiled. "Good night, Charlie," she whispered, kissed his forehead and then she turned for the door.

Downstairs, Captain Gordon and his daughter had retired to the den where Maria sat reading a book, and the captain sat in his chair pondering the incident with the broken glass and the boy's behavior. "Maria," he said quietly. "Do you think this boy could have been badly mistreated at the school?"

"Why do you ask, Papa?"

"By the way he expected to be beaten, when he broke the glass. I mean, do you suppose that it's just this one boy that is so terribly misbehaved?"

Maria had not yet spoken to anyone about what she had witnessed earlier that day when she saw the boy naked, because that would have been a great embarrassment to her. But now that her father had asked, she would find some way to justify why she, a sophisticated young lady of twenty, had been viewing the naked body of a twelve-year-old boy. "He has scars on his back," she said, looking up from her book.

"What kind of scars?" the captain asked.

"Like... marks made by a whip."

"And just how do you know this?"

"Oh, Papa," cried Maria. "I know it was wrong, but I... I happened to see him without his clothes as he was getting into his bath this afternoon. It was purely an accident that I saw him, Papa... please believe me."

"There, there, Maria. You did nothing wrong. He's just a child needing someone to care for him. It would be no different than if we had reared him from infancy. You would have bathed him many times over."

"Thank you, Papa, for understanding."

"Okay, my dear. Now tell me about the scars."

"He even admitted it. He said this nurse—he called her Mother Champlain, I believe—would put ointment on his back for him after he had been punished."

"And did he mention who had administered the

punishment?"

"No, Papa. And I didn't ask. And I don't think you should ask him either."

"Just the same, I believe that I will have a talk with Mr. Stanley about it... just the same."

That night about eleven o'clock when Maria went up to bed she couldn't resist steeling softly into Charles' bedroom, where the moonlight through the window allowed her to notice the sparkle on his cheek. *Poor child,* she thought. *He's been crying.*

She leaned over him and kissed his forehead. Her presence must have influenced his dreams. He moaned a little whimper and smiled.

At that moment Maria became aware that her father was at the door looking on. The next moment she was in his arms.

"Bless you, my dear," he said softly. "I took this on as my challenge, so that I might give you a brother, and that I might have a son. And it seems that this poor little ignorant fellow with his rough ways has roused some strong feelings."

"Yes," Maria whispered. "He needs us. And I think we need him."

Maria had been right—Charles had cried himself to sleep, feeling in his inexperienced fashion that he had failed to please the captain; that he had disgraced himself; that Mr. Stanley was right— he was truly a bad boy; that he would soon be returned to the harsh environment of the orphanage.

Circumstances, however, were influencing his future in ways he could not yet dream of.

# Chapter 15

*C*aptain Gordon laid down his pen on the desk when Maria and Charles came into the den. The boy was dressed this morning in more casual-looking clothes—a nicely-pressed white shirt and crisp blue denim trousers—although to him they seemed a bit stiff and scratchy, still not accustomed to the newness. His golden hair was neatly combed and a sheepish smile dimpled his cheeks.

"Ah, good morning, my dear," the captain said to Maria, and then gazed at the boy. "And don't you look just like a little gentleman this morning? Did you sleep well, Charles?"

"Oh, yes sir," Charles beamed. "You should see that bed up in my... er... th' room where I slept. It is *so* big and soft."

Gordon chuckled. "Yes, my boy, I *have* seen that bed."

"We have been filling Charles' dresser drawers with his new things, and hanging his shirts and trousers," Maria said.

Charles put his hand on Maria's arm but kept his eyes on Mr. Gordon. "Yeah, such a lot of things, an' she said that room is to be *my* room... all th' time. Is that so?"

Gordon smiled. "Yes, son, that is very true."

"Papa," Maria said impatiently. "I have some errands to do in town. Is it alright if Charles stays here with you for a while?"

"Why, of course, my dear." He glanced down at Charles. "You can sit here in the den and amuse yourself with a book while I finish my reports." He turned back to the papers on his desk and picked up his pen.

Charles peered around the room at the many books lined up on the shelves that occupied nearly two walls. Then he looked at Maria again. "Can't I just go with you?" he whined.

"Not now, Charles," Maria replied. "I will be very busy with things you would not enjoy at all."

Charles' expression drooped like a wilted flower.

"Later on," Maria said as she knelt by him. "When I come back, we'll go for a long walk by the river, okay?"

"Okay," he said, still sounding quite crestfallen, and he turned and plodded over to the book shelf.

Maria stood and called to her father. "I will see you in about two or three hours."

Mr. Gordon briefly glanced up from his work and gave a little wave as Maria turned and disappeared through the doorway.

Charles stared at the books, just as he had done so many times at the school. There were more books here than at the school, but they certainly didn't appear to be the kind of books he could enjoy. After taking several down from the shelf, he finally found one with many pictures. He sat down on a chair, opened the book on his knees and flipped through the pages, carefully studying the various scenes of landscapes from around the world. Quite some time had passed when he raised his eyes to have a good long look at Mr. Gordon as he sat frowning in deep thought, and scribing a few words on the paper every now and then.

He wondered what the other boys at the school would be doing. Some of them would surely be tending the cows in the pasture, and some would be shoveling the manure out of the barn. Some would be working in the huge vegetable garden, and the older boys would be chopping wood and stacking it in the woodshed for the coming winter. And some would be in the classroom, reading, or learning arithmetic, or practicing writing words and sentences.

Just then the grandfather's clock across the room chimed ten o'clock. Charles looked once again at Mr. Gordon who was still concentrating on his paperwork. "What time will Maria get back," he asked, as impatient boys will do.

"In a couple of hours," Gordon responded without even lifting his eyes from the desktop. "Just keep reading your book." He went on writing with great interest.

But not so with Charles. He had lost most of his interest in the picture book. He yawned and rubbed the back of his neck. Then he reached down to try to relieve some of the pinching of one boot. With legs stretched out, his arms went up over his head waving around in little circles. All that energy wanting to be in motion.

Then he thought he would try to walk around the room with the big book balanced on his head, which he easily did. There was no challenge in that. But when he passed by the open window, his interest was drawn to the hummingbird buzzing and darting about among the flowers just outside.

"Mr. Gordon, Sir?" he called out.

"What is it, my boy? And you shouldn't be addressing me as *Mr. Gordon*... you should be calling me *Father*... or *Papa*, like Maria does."

"Alright, Sir... F-Father, Sir." It was difficult for him to say; there hadn't been quite enough time, yet, for him to fully grasp the family concept, one which he had never really known. "What I really wanted to know... is that your garden out there?"

"Yes, of course, that's my garden."

"May I go out in it?"

"Yes, of course you may," the captain said, still unaware that the boy was balancing a book on his head.

Charles returned the book to its proper place on the shelf and there was the sound of several quick footsteps. With a single bound he was through the open French window and out upon the lawn. The captain didn't notice the boy's method of exit.

And what a wonderful garden it was! All the neighbors said that Captain Gordon's was the best garden for miles around. It was filled with all sorts of flowers—columbine, bluebells, violets, roses and daffodils—growing in great clumps among clusters of white paper birch trees and arbor vitae. There were rhododendron, and cherry and apple trees. Charles wandered past a little rock-lined pond where water lilies and cattails thrived, half-surrounded by weeping willows. Neatly-trimmed elderberry shrubs bordered a stone walkway on one side, and a mass of iris and lilies and geraniums on the other. The walkway meandered to an area of more trees—maples and black walnut, and beyond that were trellises crawling with grape vines that kept hidden the less attractive vegetable garden. Behind another row of apple and plum trees stood a glass-roofed hot house and an eight-foot high stone wall that extended from either end of the hot house past some pine trees and out of Charles' line of sight. He had never seen the likes of such a magnificent, beautiful garden. The simple vegetable garden in which he had often worked at the school was nothing compared to this.

"I wonder what is on the other side of that wall," he mumbled to himself as he gawked at the massive rock structure. His eyes surveyed the top of the wall to where it turned abruptly and tapered downward following the angle of the hot house roof to a height of about four feet. With his strength and agility he could easily scale that wall, and discover what lay beyond.

# Chapter 16

"*W*ell, lookee there!" exclaimed James, watching the boy from behind a grape vine trellis. He had been busy pulling some weeds in the cucumber patch and didn't notice the stranger as he passed by on the walkway. Mr. Gordon's gardener, James Wilkins, took much pride in the garden, and because he did most of the work maintaining it, he considered it *his* garden, and Captain Gordon was just someone he allowed to walk through it and admire it whenever he took a notion to do so. But of course, if it weren't for Maria, there wouldn't be so gosh-darn many flowers, some of which grew among the vegetables and fruit trees. He considered them a nuisance when he had to negotiate around them to get to his apples and plums that grew by the bushel and his strawberries and raspberries that were surpassed by no other in the entire county.

James could tolerate Helen's passion for herbs in the vegetable garden, but he still found plenty to grumble about, like blight and birds. "It's the blightiest garden I ever did see," he'd complain. "And a man might spend all his life keeping the birds down with a gun."

But James did not spend any part of his life keeping

the birds down with a gun. The captain caught him shooting one day. "How dare you, James?" he yelled. "I will not have a single bird destroyed on this property!"

"Then you won't get any fruit, 'cause the birds will get it all," James had responded.

"Without the birds, sir, we will be overrun with slugs and snails and harmful insects. No sir, you will not harm the birds. Is that clear, Mr. Wilkins?"

So naturally, Maria was ever so grateful to her father for protecting her beloved creatures, and in season they brightened every day with color and song.

But right now, James was not concerned about the birds. He was agitated by another creature—a strange boy dressed in pretty clothes who climbed to the top of the rock wall as easily as would a cat. Finally, he knew why some of his fruit had disappeared. He was about to catch, red-handed, the culprit that was stealing his apples and plumbs. If only Mr. Gordon had not banned the use of his gun, he'd take the thief down with a single shot.

Charles was unaware that he was being watched, nor was he concerned that his peer would be a potential enemy. He sat on his heels, holding his balance with his hands atop the wall gazing at the quiet, lazy little river some distance on the other side. Across the river he saw tamarack, jack pine, and blueberry bushes.

"Who is that boy?" James mumbled. "Never seen him before. Must be some city kid come out here to steal my apples." He grabbed a bean pole from the garden and began his stealth approach to the wall, concealing himself behind the plum trees. Then he couldn't believe his eyes when the mystery boy got on all fours, scooted down the wall a good distance, turned, and with the grace of a circus

84

performer, kicked his heels up into the air so he was standing on his hands, then *walked* on his hands back toward the hot house.

"He's gonna fall and break his fool neck," James mumbled. But then he saw the boy get back to his feet, and he rushed to the wall to intercept the intruder before he could get away. Poking at the boy with the bean pole, he yelled: "You git down from there, right now, you thievin' little tomcat! D'ya hear? Come down, I say! I should kill ya for stealin' my apples!"

Charles, to say the least, was startled... and frightened. A crazy man with a big stick wanted to kill him! But he felt somewhat trapped there on top of the wall. It was too dangerous to jump off the other side as there were jagged rocks and boulders below. The man didn't look like he was capable of climbing up the wall after him, so the best thing to do was wait. Maybe the lunatic would give up and leave. All the while the man kept poking the stick at him and yelling. But then it appeared as though the man was going to try to climb the wall. Charles looked to his right. He could easily jump to the peak of the hot house, cross over to the wall on the other end, and be gone before the man realized where he had gone. It seemed like a simple solution.

He jumped to the roof peak. He turned to see how far the man had progressed. But the man had seen his move, and was backing down off the wall. Charles knew he had little time to make his way across the roof to the other wall. He started stepping cautiously along the peak. Confidence in his sense of balance would see him through this predicament, he was certain.

Then, suddenly the man shouted at him. "Git down

from there, you little rat!" He was still waving the bean pole in the air as if it was a spear and he was a savage warrior, thirsty for blood. This interrupted Charles' concentration of balance. His foot slipped and went crashing through one of the glass roof panels. The next thing he knew, *he* was falling through the window frame, luckily now void of its glass. But he managed to catch himself with his arms wrapped around the rafters on each side, and there he hung, suspended with his bare feet dangling inside the greenhouse.

# *Chapter 17*

*C*aptain Gordon did not realize the lapse of time when Maria opened the door to the den. "I'm back," she announced, proudly showing off her curly new hair style.

"Why, you look absolutely stunning, my dear," her father said.

Maria gazed around the room. "Where's Charles?"

"The boy. Yes... well... I thought he was here."

Just then the tinkling of breaking glass was heard, and immediately following was the gruff shouts of James, the gardener: "Here! You just come down from there!"

The captain leaped to his feet and rushed to the open window, Maria on his heels. "Wilkins," he shouted. "What is going on out there?"

"I've caught me a thief," was the gardener's response. "You'd better come quick!"

"Better stay here, my dear," the captain said. "Could be danger." He quickly headed for the door out to the garden.

But this was one time that Maria decided to disobey her father. She suspected something entirely different from what the gardener was claiming. Following closely behind the captain, they hurried down the pathway to the hot house where the shouts were coming from.

"Ah... glad you're here," said James. "Finally got one of 'em."

"One of what?" said Gordon in a disgusted tone.

"One o' them scoundrels tryin' t' steal our fruit."

"Oh! Papa! Look!" cried Maria, pointing to the roof.

"Why, Charles," the captain called out. He stared

wildly at the boy, bare feet and legs kicking, searching blindly for some support. "What on earth are you doing up there?" he snarled.

"It's all right," the boy said calmly. "Only one pane broke."

James scratched his head, confused. The captain seemed to know this boy.

"How did you ever get into such a position?" cried Maria.

"Couldn't help it," Charles answered. "That crazy man there was after me with that big stick, tryin' to kill me."

Gordon glared at James. "Is this so?" he said angrily.

"Well, yes, sir, I s'pose it is," said the gardener. "Y' see, I seen him up on the wall... figured he'd come stealin' apples. Told him t' come down, but he wouldn't... and then he fell through the hot house winder."

"Did ya' think I was gonna come down when you was swingin' at me with that big stick?" Charles called out.

"You had no business up on our wall," James said. "Now look at the damage you've done."

"That will be quite enough, Wilkins," Gordon said sternly.

"But I didn't know it was someone you knew," James said in his defense.

"No, of course you didn't."

"Ah... ain't somebody gonna help me get down," Charles said in desperation.

"Oh, yes," Gordon said. "Keep still so you don't cut yourself."

"I already have cut myself, and it's bleeding," said the boy. "D'ya s'pose somebody could get a ladder?"

"Wilkins!" shouted the captain. "Go to the tool shed

and get a fruit ladder!  Hurry!"

Maria cried in sympathy.  "Are you hurt badly, Charles?"

"I d'know," he replied.  "Hurts a little bit.  Is that crazy man coming back soon with th' ladder?"

"Yes, Charles, he is," said Maria.  "And I'm sure he didn't mean to harm you.  You're a good boy."

Charles smiled down at her.  "No, I ain't.  I try to be.  But I ain't a good boy.  I broke this here window.  S'pose I'll get the switch this time, for sure."

Maria didn't answer.  She didn't know what to say.

Charles saw James coming with the ladder long before Maria and the captain knew he was near.  "Here he comes, and I'm glad, because my arms are starting to hurt."

"Hang on, Charles," Gordon said.  "We'll get you down real soon."

James leaned the ladder against the rafter and held it tight, so as not to let it slip.  Charles found a rung with one foot and managed to support his weight well enough to let go with one arm, and then cautiously stepped down the ladder.  When he reached the bottom, James stepped away and Gordon was there waiting with a stern frown.

"I'm very sorry, sir," Charles said.

"You rascal," 'Gordon said, seizing the boy's shoulder with a firm grip.  "Where is you jacket, and where are your boots?" he asked, staring down at the boy's bare feet.

"I didn't have a jacket, sir, and my boots are under a little cedar by the pond."

"Well then, let's fetch them and go back to the house."

# Chapter 18

*I*n the house, Mr. Gordon examined the boy's arms. The cuts were not severe, no more than scratches, and the bleeding had already stopped.

"Now Charles," he said, looking the boy straight in his eyes. "I suppose you know that I am very much displeased."

"Yes, sir. I don't wonder a bit. Do I get the switch now?"

Gordon bit his lip. "No, not now. But I want you to go to your room and get washed up. Put on some clean clothes, and then come back down."

Charles glanced at Maria, but she looked away. He went slowly to his room.

When they were alone, Gordon said: "I'm afraid I shall have to send him back to the school."

Maria fixed her gaze on him.

"I expected him to be a little rough," he continued. "But it seems that he is just too wild. What do you think, my dear? He's too bad to keep?"

After a few moments of silence, Maria spoke softly. "Yes, there are some things about the boy that are distasteful. But on the other hand, I can't help but like him."

"Yes, I know. Sometimes I think he deserves a good thrashing, but I know I could never lay a hand on him. Oh, what should I do? Send him back?"

"No, Papa. If you intend to adopt a boy, this is the one you are meant to have. I think he *is* a good boy inside, and that good boy deserves a chance to show himself."

Just then Helen came in and announced that lunch was ready and waiting in the dining room, and Charles appeared. He was clean and dressed properly.

"May I have some lunch, too?" he asked shyly. "I am so very hungry."

"Yes, of course. But do you have anything else to say?"

"Well, sir, I'm very sorry about breaking that window. I was afraid of the crazy man chasing me with that big stick. I wasn't doing anything wrong when he came after me. Please believe me."

"Yes, I understand. But I have been discussing with Maria about sending you back to the Mission School."

"Sending me back, sir?"

"Yes. I want a good boy; you have been quite a rascal."

"I don't want to be bad," the boy cried. "Honest."

Maria couldn't bear the anguish any longer. She put her hands on the boy's shoulders and steered him toward the dining room. "Come, Charles. Let's go have our lunch."

Charles ate very little of the baked chicken, even though he had been quite hungry. He saw the disappointment in Maria's eyes, but he didn't realize it was her disliking of her father's actions that made her frown. When he had eaten all he could, he asked to be excused so that he might go to his room.

Helen escorted him from the dining room, whispered in his ear, "Everything will be alright," and then immediately returned to the dining table.

"Mr. Gordon, sir, with all due respect, may I give you a bit of motherly advice?"

"Please do."

"I helped you raise your daughter to be a fine young lady."

"That you did, Helen, and I am most grateful."

"I have been watching the proceedings with this young boy. Did you not bring him into your home to show him the value of family? And to make him a gentleman by virtue of good family life?"

"I did, indeed."

"And did you not vow to be a good father to him, and show him love and affection?"

"Y-yes, I did."

"Well, don't you realize that this boy has never known what those values are supposed to be? Fine clothes and a comfortable bed are important, but he needs more than that. He needs something more than scolding. Everything that has happened to make him look bad has been because someone or something pushed him in the wrong directions. The broken water glass happened only because he was nervous and uncomfortable with your lecturing him about how to eat his supper. And today, he was just being a boy. Boys explore new and unfamiliar territory. They go barefoot, and climb, and spend their energy. That's all he did. And then James came along and frightened him into breaking the window. The boy didn't do anything wrong. It's all of us who have been wrong. So far, Mr. Gordon, you haven't shown him what a father really is. And Maria is absolutely right—he is a good boy inside, and he deserves a chance. And one more thing—if you decide that he should stay, try calling him *Charlie*. He likes that. I know."

Reluctantly, Mr. Gordon smiled. He knew Helen was right. He knew Maria had made an accurate evaluation of the boy. *Charlie was here to stay.*

# Chapter 19

*C*aptain Gordon spent a great deal of time away from home during the summer months. His employer, the McDonald Brothers, Black River logging magnates, as well as the owners of a riverboat fleet, kept him busy piloting on the Mississippi. Capable pilots were in demand, and therefore were paid quite well—the highest-paid profession of the day.

Charlie Martin settled into his new lifestyle, exercising great effort to avoid activities that might entice a boy into mischief—which included just about everything. He was quite certain that the gardener, James Wilkins, did not like him after the incident involving the wall and the hot house window that he fell through. So the only time he dared venture out into the garden was when Maria would accompany him; they would go for long walks out past the barrier wall where they could access the riverbank. Charlie particularly enjoyed strolling there, for there was a part of him, deep inside, that seemed somewhat familiar with the more natural terrain, and he felt comfortable with it. Not that he disliked the nicely groomed garden—he loved that too. But he never knew when Mr. Wilkins might be lurking about.

Occasionally, while exploring the riverbank, Charlie saw other boys fishing along the opposite side of the little river. They seemed to be enjoying the activity, and Charlie knew he would enjoy it, too... if he were allowed to do it.

One of Mr. Stanley's assistants at the Mission School had taken the boys in small groups on fishing excursions several times to a much smaller stream where they caught a few trout. Charlie caught only one, and it was rather small, but at least he had *some* experience. And how much mischief could he possibly get into by fishing?

In time, Maria tired of the walks along the river; she would stay in the garden and admire her beautiful flowers and take in all the fragrances. Every day she would cut a bouquet of fresh blossoms for the house, and meanwhile, she would send Charlie off on his own to enjoy the riverbank.

After several days of noticing the same boy across the river, he decided that this must be a good spot—for the same boy to return every day—and he thought he would ask Maria if she could help him acquire some fishing gear.

"Papa will be home soon," she said. "You'd better ask him."

Later that evening when Captain Gordon arrived, he appeared exhausted and informed Helen that he didn't need any supper, that he had already eaten aboard the boat with his crew. He only wanted a small glass of brandy with his coffee in the den, and then he would go to bed, as he had to rise early the next morning; awaiting his boat was another raft of logs and lumber to be towed down the Mississippi to Dubuque.

While he sipped his coffee, Charlie came into the den and stood at his side.

"Well, there's my boy!" the captain said. "How are you getting along?"

"Very well, sir," Charlie replied with a grin. But then a slight frown of disappointment took away the smile. "Miss

Helen says you have to leave again early in the morning."

"Yes, I'm afraid so, Charlie. 'Tis a busy time on the river right now."

"May I come with you on your boat, Sir?"

The captain smiled, proud that his adopted son was showing some desire to spent time with him. After all, it had been his intension to eventually teach Charlie to be a river pilot. "Someday... when you're a little older," he said. "Maybe when you grow a little more, Mr. McDonald will let me bring you on as a deckhand... to start."

"Okay," the boy said. He didn't know what a deckhand was, but he liked the sound of it. "But what I really came to ask you..."

"Yes, Charlie. What is it?"

"Well, I want to go fishing in that little river down behind the wall. But Maria said I have to wait for you."

"Do you know how to fish?"

"Oh, yes, sir. Otto used to take us boys from the school fishing. He taught me. I caught a dandy trout once."

"Well, then. I don't see any reason that you can't go fishing."

"But I don't have a pole... or line... or hooks."

"Well, I used to do some fishing, and there's a nice cane pole and everything you might need out in the carriage house. I'll set it out for you before I leave. It all belongs to you now."

"Oh, thank you, Sir!" Charlie beamed with joy. He was about to do cartwheels around the room, but then he thought better of it.

"And you know, Charlie," Gordon continued. "Fish don't usually bite after an empty hook."

"No, Sir, they don't," the boy replied. He had been

contemplating that as his next obstacle.

"I'm sure if you ask James, he will help you dig up some worms."

"But Mr. James doesn't like me, Sir."

"Oh, nonsense. You ask him in the morning."

The next morning during breakfast Charlie excitedly told Maria about the gift of all the fishing gear from the captain. She seemed quite delighted at first, that Charlie finally had an activity of his own. She had scolded him for throwing stones, when she finally realized that the birds were the targets of his favorite pastime. He had promised not to, but she feared that he still might torment the creatures when he was out of her view. So, with fishing occupying his time, maybe he wouldn't bother the birds anymore.

Then an expression of worry crept onto her face. Fishing, for all practical purposes, should be a harmless activity, but considering Charlie's past record, she wondered if he needed supervision. But her father had given his approval.

After breakfast Charlie darted out to find the cane pole, recalling the instructions and advice he had received from Otto, who had been a fisherman all his life, the river and streams always holding more attraction for him than work. It was a well-known fact that he always knew where to find the fish, but Charlie could not rely on him now for that information. He was on his own.

He discovered the cane pole and all the tackle that Mr. Gordon had promised. It was a splendid bamboo pole, with strong silk line, a cork float glistening with blue and white paint, and at least a dozen extra hooks in a square metal can with a lid. He had everything he needed except bait, and he was not particularly fond of seeking the gardener for help. He thought about finding a spade and digging for worms himself, but the consequences of turning over a bit of soil in James' garden without his permission could be much worse.

James saw the boy coming, but he pretended not to notice and went about his business of cutting dead leaves and branches from the High Bush Cranberry shrubs. "What mischief is he up to now?" he grumbled under his breath, and then he became aware that the boy was searching for him. Avoidance was no longer an option, as Charlie had already spotted him.

"Hi, Mr. James, sir," Charlie said boldly.

The gardener just grunted.

"Would you please help me dig some worms?"

"Ain't got time t' be bothered..." he said gruffly. He hesitated. "Worms?"

"Yes, sir," said Charlie. "I'm goin' fishing, and I want some worms... red ones... please?"

Then James changed his tone, as he, too, had a weakness for the line and hook. "Going fishing?"

"Yes, if I can find some worms."

"Alright. I'll dig you some. Go behind the grape vines, there, by the cucumber patch. Got a pot?"

Charlie shook his head.

"Alright," said James. "I'll get one."

Charlie waited by the cucumbers, and in a few minutes James returned with a five-tined fork and an old flower pot. Because the boy was a fellow angler suddenly seemed to supersede any former ill-feelings. He raked away some dry straw that covered the bare ground and then turned over a few big clumps of the moist soil, displaying plenty of wiggling red worms suitable for baiting a fishhook.

"There you are," James said after they had put a little bit of dirt and an ample supply of worms in the pot. He winked at the boy. "Now you can go fishing. There's a deep hole up near the end of the wall." Right then, James decided that *maybe* the boy wasn't *all* bad.

"Thank you, Mr. James, sir." And right then, Charlie decided that James Wilkins, the gardener, wasn't such a bad fellow after all.

# Chapter 20

*C*harlie hurried down to the riverbank, found the spot that James had suggested, and for the next few minutes, in the shade of a large oak tree, he was busy fitting his tackle. All the while there was that same boy he had seen there many times before, squatting on the opposite bank and staring intensely at his fish line in the water before him, and by the time Charlie had baited his hook, the other boy had pulled in two silvery fish.

The river was only about forty feet wide at that point, and as Charlie prepared his line and hook, he watched the boy across the river, and he knew the boy was watching him, too.

He was dark-haired, dark-skinned, like he had spent his whole life baking in the sun, shabbily-dressed, and instead of a bamboo fishing pole and shiny float he used a rough hickory affair, and his float was just a common piece of wood. Before Charlie was ready to put his line in the water, the shabby-looking boy had caught another fish.

Charlie's heart beat faster with anticipation as at last he threw out his line as far as he could. The float and the baited hook splashed into the water, and the boy on the opposite bank chuckled.

"Why is he laughing at me?" Charlie mumbled to himself. He experimented with trying to watch the other boy with one eye and his float with the other, but that did not work so well, and he found himself gazing from one to the other, always quickly back at the float thinking that it had bobbed.

But the float did nothing but float and its only movement was from the ripples as the boy on the other side jerked his pole, making another strike, and pulled onto the bank yet another fish. In a nonchalant manner, Charlie lifted his line out of the water and swung it toward the bank, only to notice that the worm was gone. Trying to be very casual, conscious of the other boy watching him with critical eyes, he renewed the bait and threw it in again. But there was no bite, and as time went on, it seemed as all the fish had been attracted to the other side of the river where the shabby-looking boy skillfully brought in several more. Granted, they were not huge fish, but they *were* fish.

After another hour, the dark-skinned boy across the river wound the line around his crude wooden pole. He waved and smiled to Charlie as he picked up his basket of fish, briskly making his way along the bank among the jack pines. He stopped to pick a few blueberries, and then he went on. Charlie watched him until he was nearly out of sight, but then the boy thrust a canoe out from the bank, climbed into it, and paddled down the river.

"He's an Indian boy," Charlie said upon seeing the canoe. "No wonder he's such a good fisherman." Then he pondered some more. "If he comes back again, I'll talk to him. I'll find out his secret... how he catches so many fish."

Every morning for the next three days, Charlie hurried to the riverbank with his bamboo pole and flower pot of worms, expecting the Indian boy to return. But the bank on the other side of the river remained void of any fishermen. He had not made acquaintance with that Indian boy, but nonetheless, he felt lonely without him there. He continued to dangle his line in the river with not much more than an occasional nibble, and only once did a sucker take his hook. But he recognized it as a fish not worth taking home—Otto had taught him that—and so he removed it from the hook and threw it back into the river.

Three days of fishing without catching a single keeper can be quite discouraging for any angler, and for Charlie, this was no exception. On Saturday morning, the fourth day, he sat on the steps gazing out at the garden in despair when Maria came out, ready to find a fresh bouquet. She stopped, observed Charlie's gloomy expression, and sat down beside him. "Why, Charlie," she said. "You look quite unhappy today. Are you bored with the fishing already?"

"Well, the fish just aren't biting. I haven't caught a single one worth keeping. I *so* wanted to bring home a good fish dinner for us."

Maria gently caressed his shoulder with her hand. "Maybe the fish weren't hungry for the last few days. Maybe today they are, and today will be your day to catch some."

"D'ya really think so?"

"Sure! I hate to see you so sad. Why don't you go give it another try?"

With a little renewed spirit of encouragement, Charlie found his pole, trudged off to the cucumber patch where James helped him find some fresh worms, and headed toward the end of the wall to the river. After a few minutes of just staring into the water, a reflection caught his eye. It was the reflection of the Indian boy on the opposite bank. Charlie beamed a big smile and waved. The boy returned the greeting.

Charlie went about baiting his hook, and the Indian boy did the same. Within five minutes, the boy across the river struck at a bite and pulled in a fish. Charlie sat and watched his motionless float, working up the courage to call out to the other boy.

When the boy had landed another fish, Charlie finally said: "You sure are lucky!"

The boy smiled, baited his hook, and threw it out again, and just a few minutes later, he was pulling in another fish.

"You sure are lucky!" Charlie called out again.

"Not so much luck," the boy said, his voice easily passing over the water. "You baiting with red worms?"

"Yes, I surely am," Charlie answered.

"Well, I think you're not fishing deep enough," said the Indian boy.

"I ain't?"

"No. Put a little more line below your float... about two more feet."

Charlie thought he had arranged his tackle just the way Otto had taught him, but then he remembered that was when they were fishing for trout in a much smaller, shallower stream. He hauled in his line, attached the float to his line like the boy had told him, and tossed the baited hook back in the water. Sure enough, in about four minutes, Charlie felt a little tug on his line and the float bobbed repeatedly.

"Why don't you strike at it?" the Indian boy shouted.

"I don't think he has the hook yet," Charlie replied, a little excitement in his voice.

"Strike!" the boy yelled again.

Charlie jerked the pole, but up came an empty hook. He swung it back toward him, put on another worm, and tossed it back in the water. Meanwhile, the Indian boy had hooked another one, baited his hook and was patiently waiting for another bite.

Again, there was another sharp tug on Charlie's line.

"There! You've got another bite!" the Indian boy called out. "Look at him... he's trying to run away with it."

Little credit could have been given to Charlie for striking at this one at the right moment, as the unfortunate smallmouth bass had hooked itself. It darted back and forth below the surface, racing as far as the line would allow in one direction, and then the other, trying to escape. More than once Charlie almost lost his grip on the bamboo pole, his eyes widening with astonishment and disbelief as the big fish flew out of the water, momentarily suspended in mid-air, showing its size, and then splashed down again. Finally the creature tired and gave up the battle. Charlie hauled in the line, and this time he had the prize he'd been after.

"Magnifique, mon ami!" cried the boy from across the river. "What a fine fish!"

Charlie had been admiring the five-pound bass that lay at his feet in the grass, and then the boy's words registered. He glanced at the boy on the far bank who he thought to be Indian, but he remembered some of the boys at the Mission School who used those French words in their speech, of which he had learned the English translation by living with them for so long. But this boy didn't look anything like those French boys at the school.

Then the boy across the river called out again. "Au revoir, mon ami! No more fish will we catch today," he said as he waved and headed downriver to his canoe.

"Wait!" yelled Charlie. "Will you be back?"

"Oui, mon ami," the boy replied. "Yes, my friend, I shall return tomorrow afternoon... but on *your* side of the river."

Charlie nearly burst with pride as he displayed the big fish to Maria and Helen back at the house. "May we eat it for supper?" he asked Helen.

"Well, bless your heart, Charlie Martin!" Helen cried. There was no doubt that she was impressed with the catch. She took the fish from Charlie. "You certainly may," she said. "I'll have James clean it and cut it into fillets. It will make a fine supper for you and Maria."

"You see, Charlie?" Maria said. "I knew you would have better luck today."

He said nothing about the French-speaking Indian boy from across the river.

# Chapter 21

$S$unday morning had always been a time of worship for the Gordon household.  But Maria had not attended church services for a while, since her father had to be gone on the river most of the time, and she wasn't comfortable with taking Charlie with her until she felt certain he would not embarrass her.  Now that he had gone many weeks without serious incident, mainly because she had devoted most of her time to his conditioning and steering him away from his schoolboy chatter to a more gentlemanly manner of speech, Maria decided to bravely risk public opinion; they should go.  Charlie wasn't extremely pleased with the idea, but he took his bath and dressed in his finest—starched white shirt with turned down collar, black tie, and waist coat, even though the weather was still quite hot.

James drove them to the church in the best carriage on that pleasant morning.  When they arrived, the widow Mrs. Wood met them in the churchyard. "Well, good morning, Miss Gordon," she greeted.  She gazed down at Charlie. "And this must be the captain's protégé."

Maria smiled.  "Yes, this is Charles Martin," she said, and then introduced Mrs. Wood.  "Charles, Mrs. Wood is a sister of Papa's best friend and colleague, Frank McIntyre. He's a riverboat pilot, too."

Charlie dimpled his cheeks with a boyish smile and bowed his head as a gesture of courtesy, like Maria had taught him, and then gazed around at all the people entering the church while the two women chatted some more.

"What did she mean?" Charlie asked when Mrs. Wood had walked away.

"Who? Mrs. Wood?"

"Why did she look sorry for me and call me a *potato jay?*"

Maria giggled. "Protégé—it's a French word for someone who is adopted or protected... like Papa is protecting you."

"Well, why did she laugh? Is that funny?"

Maria couldn't answer. She only recalled in her mind the conversation that her father had had with Frank about raising a gentleman from a lowly orphan. She tried to put it out of her thoughts as she guided the boy into the church.

She was thankful when the closing hymn had concluded, as Charlie had been quite restless all during the service. He participated nicely by singing the hymns and praying the *Lord's Prayer,* but just as young boys will, he was anxious to be on the move. Outside while the parishioners mingled and chatted in small groups, and while Maria and Charlie waited for James to pick them up again, Preacher Hornsby strolled toward them. "Ah, Miss Gordon... so good to see you here today. And who's this?" he asked, pretending not to recognize the boy. He visited the Mission School weekly, instructed Catechism to the children there, and had been one of the first to know about Captain Gordon's adoption. "Oh, yes," he said, raising his eye glasses to his face. "It's the captain's young protégé. Yes... I remember you now... and I suppose you remember me."

"Yes, I remember you," said Charlie. "You called me a stupid boy because I couldn't remember all of the *Apostle's Creed.*"

"Did I?" the preacher said, a little taken aback. "But you are not stupid now," he said in a guarded, lower tone, hoping that no one else overheard the boy's statement. "I dare say that you now remember every word."

"I don't think so," the boy replied honestly. "It's still hard to remember *every* word."

Maria turned a bright shade of red.

"But I'm not going to ask you to recite it now," said the preacher. "Miss Gordon will help you with it, I'm sure." He shook hands with both of them and nodded as they turned and walked to the gate where they stepped aboard their waiting carriage.

# Chapter 22

*C*harlie was quite anxious to get back to the river. The Indian boy would surely return, and he was the closest thing to a playmate Charlie had seen since he left the Mission School, although he did not miss the other boys there so much. The Indian boy spoke kindly to him and offered him friendship—something he had not seen much of at the school. But his biggest fear was that Maria and the captain would not approve of this friend because he was shabby-looking, so for now, he would keep his new-found friend a secret.

More than an hour passed while Charlie sat on the riverbank waiting for the mysterious boy to arrive. He thought about baiting his hook and tossing the line in the water, but it was such a pleasant day to just soak up the warm sunshine; there was scarcely a cloud in the sky. Birds sang and the scent of the jack pines drifted on a faint breeze.

"Why aren't you fishing?" a voice asked, and then Charlie realized he had been daydreaming. He hadn't noticed the Indian boy walking along the bank from where he had landed his canoe downstream.

"Oh! Hi," Charlie said. "Um... just got here. Nice day, isn't it?"

And so there they sat, that very mismatched pair, fishing on the bank of the La Crosse River, caring not much about anything else right then. The fish weren't biting, but it didn't seem to matter as they sat in silence, every now and then stealing a glance at each other.

After quite some time, there came a little bob to the Indian boy's wooden float. He gave a tug on the line, but an empty hook came out of the water. He put on another worm and threw it back in.

A couple of minutes later, Charlie's cork float bobbed, and then suddenly glided away beneath the surface. It took him by such surprise; he gave a tremendous jerk with his rod. The fish came sailing out of the water and up among the low, overhanging tree branches. The line caught there, and the fish hung suspended about a foot below a cluster of twigs, frantically flipping about, trying to get itself free.

The Indian boy burst into a roar of laughter, stamped his feet and slapped his knees, while Charlie stood with his pole in hand, tugging at the line.

"You'll break the line," the Indian boy said.

"But I want to get the fish down."

"You shouldn't have struck so hard. You'll have to climb out on that branch to get it."

Charlie stared at the tree for a moment, its branches extending out over the water. Then he stared at the water that looked frightfully deep and dark.

"Who taught you how to fish?" the Indian boy asked.

"Why, it was Otto, at the..." Charlie stopped short. He realized then that he was, perhaps, a little embarrassed to admit that he had lived nearly his entire life at the orphanage, even to this boy who he hardly knew.

"You mean Otto Simonton?" the boy asked.

"Yes, that's him," Charlie said. "D'ya know him?"

"Sure, I know him. We have fished together many

times on the Mississippi. But I can't imagine Otto teaching you to chuck a fish up into a tree."

"He didn't. That part was sort of an accident."

"Say," the Indian boy said. "If it was Otto you been fishing with, are you one of them from the Mission School?"

Charlie's stare dropped to his feet. "Yeah... I used to live there."

"Oui... I see you there sometimes when I take the cows from town out to pasture. What's your name?"

"Charles Martin Gordon. But everybody now just calls me Charlie."

The Indian boy stepped closer and held out his right hand. "Pleased to meet you, mon ami, Charlie."

They shook hands and then the boy continued: "My name is Dominic Bouton."

Charlie gave the boy a peculiar stare. "You use so many French words, but you look..."

"Like an Indian?" Dominic finished the statement.

"Well... yeah."

"My father and two half-brothers are French, and living in that house, I learned the French ways. But my mother was Winnebago, and they say I inherited her dark skin and hair. That's why I sound French and look like an Indian."

"And you're so good at fishing. Did Otto teach you?"

"No, no, mon ami. My Winnebago uncle, Gray Wolf taught me how to hunt and fish."

Charlie glanced up to the tree branch where his line was caught and the fish still hung, and then he turned back to Dominic and grinned. "Guess Gray Wolf was a better teacher, huh."

They both laughed.

"I could teach you," Dominic said. "I know all the good places to fish."

"Could you?" Charlie said, awed by such an offer.

"Of course I could, any day... except Wednesday, Thursday, or Friday. Those days I tend the cows and earn my money."

"Earn your money?"

"Oui... to buy food."

"But doesn't your father buy your food?"

"My father is gone," said Dominic. And then, as if he was trying to avoid any further conversation about his father, he nodded toward Charlie's marooned fish line in the tree. "Gonna climb up there and get your line down?"

Charlie examined the tree once more, laid down his pole on the bank, and with determination in his eyes he began the climb. He quickly reached the limb protruding out over the water—the one that had entangled his line.

"That's it," said Dominic, watching from below as Charlie inched his way out along the branch. "Only four more feet and you should be able to reach the line."

Charlie couldn't see the line or the fish for the bushy foliage, so he had to rely on Dominic's guidance.

"It's about a foot in front of you," Dominic called out.

Charlie probed with one hand, hanging onto the branch and maintaining his balance with the other. When he finally found the line, it was too tangled to free with one hand.

"Have a knife?" said Dominic.

"Yes, in my pocket," replied Charlie.

"Maybe you can cut the small branches off... let it all drop down into the water. Then I can haul it in for you."

Charlie thought that was a reasonable solution, but it was not so easy getting the knife from his pocket, or opening the blade, as he was hanging in a very awkward position. All the while he was struggling with the knife, it seemed as though the tree limb was sagging lower under his weight.

Finally the branch with the tangled line was cut completely through. Branch, line, and fish fell to the water, and Dominic hastily reeled it onto the bank. Charlie closed the knife, and with a little difficulty managed to get it into his pocket again.

As Charlie attempted to work his way backward on the limb, he heard an ominous cracking noise. He paused for a moment, and with his next move came another loud, splintering crack. A moment later—PA-LOOSH! Branch and Charlie hit the water with a tremendous splash and both went down out of sight.

Although he knew it was a rather unfortunate situation for Charlie, Dominic couldn't help but laugh. But then he slowly realized that Charlie wasn't coming up again. He could barely see that Charlie was free from the tree limb, but he seemed to be struggling, as if he might be injured.

Dominic quickly ripped off his shirt and trousers and dove into the dark water, and while still beneath the surface, in one smooth motion grasped Charlie around his chest and brought him to the surface, and then to the shore.

"Are you hurt, mon ami?" he asked Charlie when they were safely on solid ground.

"No, I don't think so," Charlie said, catching his breath.

"Then why—"

"I don't know how to swim."

"Little Otter will teach you."

"Little Otter? Who is Little Otter?"

"My Indian cousins call me Little Otter... because I swim under water... just like an otter."

Charlie examined his wet clothes that were now quite muddy, too, from climbing up the riverbank. "Thanks for saving me," he said. "Now I have to figure a way to save myself from Maria."

Dominic stared curiously. "Who is Maria?"

"She's... er... my sister. She'll be furious with me for ruining my clothes."

"Not if we wash them," suggested Dominic. "And while we're waiting for them to dry in the sun, I can teach you to swim."

It wasn't the worst idea, but then again, climbing out on that branch to retrieve the fish line seemed like a good idea, too, at the time. But at this point, Charlie had nothing to lose. "Okay... but under one condition," he said as he started unbuttoning his mud-stained shirt.

Dominic stared at him questioningly.

"That you promise not to let me drown."

Downstream a short way, they waded out into shallow water and scrubbed away the mud stains from Charlie's clothes, and then hung them in the tree in the afternoon sun. And for the next three hours, Charlie learned the basics of swimming. He was a fast learner when it came to physical activities, and the sport of swimming seemed to come easy. Once again, his strength and agility aided tremendously. He wasn't quite as good or as fast in the water as Dominic, yet, but with a little more training and practice he would get better.

After the strenuous workout, they sat on the bank letting the sun dry them off. When they were getting dressed, Charlie noticed the tiny leather pouch that Dominic hung around his neck. "What's that?" he asked.

Dominic clutched the little pouch in his hand and closed his eyes tightly for a moment. Then he opened his hand and looked at Charlie. "My uncle gave it to me, but it actually came from my grandfather. It is a medicine bag."

"Medicine bag?" It has medicine in it?"

"Oui, mon ami... but not the same kind of medicine you are thinking of. Indian medicine is different. It contains the good spirit of the earth, and if I keep it near me, it will drive away the bad spirits."

"You said your father was gone. Where is he?"

Dominic pointed a far-away stare out to the jack pines across the river. "I don't know," he said, his words soft and solemn. "Last year he took my brother, Louis, to Montreal. Louis was to enter Montreal College. He wanted to become a priest. But my father never came back."

Charlie thought a moment. He remembered from school lessons that Montreal was far away in Canada. "Do you think he stayed there?"

"No... his business is here. He would not stay. I fear something bad has happened to him."

"What about your mother and your other brother?"

"My mother rests in the churchyard. She has been dead four years. And Jacques... he went to the far west to become a trader, like my father, in the wilderness where many people are going now. He has been gone for more than a year."

"So... you're all alone."

"Oui."

Charlie put his arm around Dominic's shoulders. "There must be somebody who can help you."

"Why do I need help? My Indian cousins taught me to hunt and fish; I have a job to earn money for the things I cannot get from the forest; I have my canoe so I can cross the big river whenever I want. So, tell me, mon ami... why do I need help?"

"Why don't you go live with your Indian family?"

"I don't want to live like them, in huts and tepees... and nothing more than a heap of straw and a deer skin for a bed on the ground. *Mon Dieu!* I like my house and my bed."

"But... you're just a kid... like me."

"And we will soon grow, and we will survive. And you must promise one thing, Mon ami."

"What?"

"That you will tell no one who I am."

"Why not?"

"I have many friends in the town. I always speak French when I am around them so they won't think I am Indian, because many people are afraid of the Indians and think of them badly. If they find out I have Indian blood, they might not like me anymore."

Charlie pondered on the request for a few moments. It didn't seem unreasonable, and in just the past few hours, he had become quite fond of his new friend. Dominic had treated him better than anyone had ever treated him at the Mission School; he had given some good fishing advice; he had taught him how to swim. And how could he *not* honor a simple request from someone who had *saved his life?*

"Okay," said Charlie, offering to shake hands on the promise. "I won't tell anybody."

116

## *Chapter 23*
### June 1879

*C*harlie Martin had spent that entire fall, winter, and spring attending the school in La Crosse, while Dominic laid in a good supply of venison, smoked fish, and firewood, and had hunkered down in his cozy cabin on Barron's Island. They scarcely saw each other once Charlie started school.

Even with Maria's tutoring, Charlie wasn't a star pupil, not much more than average. But when the lessons were done, he listened intensely to Mr. Gordon as he talked about the river and steamboats, and told his stories about experiences with both. Captain Gordon was spending much more time at his home when the river froze, ending the shipping season on the Upper Mississippi; he and Charlie found more and more common ground as the weeks passed, and Charlie even started calling him *Captain*.

Charlie had made a few friends at his new school, but

now that summer replaced the classroom, he thought more about his Indian friend from last summer. He hadn't seen Dominic since before Thanksgiving; he didn't know where the boy lived, and because he had promised not to reveal the boy's secret, he dared not ask anyone for fear they might ask too many questions.

Charlie worried about his friend, surviving the winter all alone with no adults to take care of him. He desperately hoped that Dominic had not frozen to death in the frigid cold, or starved, or drowned in the spring flood. Perhaps he had gone to live with his Indian family—wherever that was. Or maybe his father had come back.

Dominic grew further distant from the idea that his father would ever return. His Winnebago friends and relatives from his mother's village in Northeast Iowa had stopped their journeys upriver when they learned that Henri Bouton, their trusted trader friend was not there doing business on Barron's Island. When Gray Wolf offered Dominic a home in their village, he had replied, "Thank you, Uncle, but my home is here, and this is where I will stay." He hadn't seen his Indian family since.

High water of the springtime floods had receded and Barron's Island was once again green and sweet-smelling with wild flowers and apple blossoms, as was the countryside where Dominic tended the small herd of cows, just as he had done for the past three years. Over the long, lonely winter months he had spent endless hours practicing with the flute his brother gave him, and now he could play not only the Indian melodies his mother had taught him, but many of the tunes he had heard in the town and around the riverboats at the docks. So he carried the flute with him when he took the cows to pasture; it helped pass the time, and the cows seemed more contented, too.

Charlie had gained a little more freedom from close supervision by Maria; he knew he was a handful for her, constantly being distracted from his studies by urges to attempt new acrobatic stunts, and sometimes mischievously stealing pastries from Helen's pantry. But for her he had tried harder to become more judicious, and he realized that he would always be indebted to her for taking him so far on his journey to becoming a gentleman. She had sacrificed so much of her time for him, and now the summertime was a time for her, as well as Charlie, to take a break from schoolwork and to enjoy all the great new life that spring had delivered to the garden.

Charlie was ever so grateful to the captain, too, for rescuing him from that dismal life at the orphanage school. Not that he wasn't grateful for that, too, for that place had provided him survival from an uncertain death. But Captain Gordon could offer him so much more, especially the father figure that had always been missing. Now that the captain was away much of the time with the new shipping season, Charlie missed the companionship, of which he had become so fond during the winter months. He longed to go on the boat with Captain, but Gordon had insisted that he wait another year. When he was fifteen— more educated, more refined, more seasoned—he was promised a position aboard the captain's boat, and perhaps, after a couple of years getting familiar with the river and the operation of steamboats, he could begin his training as a cub pilot. For now, though, Charlie was content with fishing and swimming in the La Crosse River, hopeful that the French-speaking Indian boy, Dominic, would return.

James, the gardener had designated particular areas where Charlie could dig for earth worms anytime he wanted to go fishing, so the boy took every opportunity to sit at the river with a line in the water. And as the weather got warmer, and if the fish weren't biting, he spent a good share of the time swimming, practicing and polishing the techniques Dominic had taught him.

And then one Saturday in mid-June while he lay back on the riverbank with one arm covering his eyes a voice yanked him from his drowsiness: "Mon ami... you can't catch fish if you don't watch your line!" He jumped to his feet and let the fish pole drop to the ground. There was Dominic sauntering up the bank toward him, a big grin on his face. Charlie sprinted to meet him and they threw their arms around each other, both glad to be together again.

"I've been worried about you," Charlie said as they pushed each other back at arm's length. "But I didn't know where to find you."

"Been fishing the trout streams... best time in the spring, y' know."

They looked each other up and down; both had grown considerably since they were last together. Unlike Charlie's bright, new, perfect-fitting clothes, Dominic was still dressed in his shabby-looking faded and ill-fitting shirt and trousers that had been handed down from his older brothers. But the appearance of their clothes meant very little, for their friendship had become much stronger than that.

They sat down on the riverbank shoulder to shoulder.

"So, you have been at the big school in town all winter," Dominic said. "Is it better than the Mission School?"

"Oh, yes... I learned ever so much, but I know I won't ever be able to remember it all." Charlie eyed his friend. "Why don't you go to school?" he asked suspiciously.

Dominic frowned and gazed down at his feet. "My father was ashamed of his little Indian boy offspring, so he never sent me to school."

"Ashamed of you!"

"Oui, mom ami. That is why Jacques and Louis were the ones to go with him on voyages to Montreal, but I always stayed at home."

"He didn't come back yet?" Charlie asked.

"No."

"Was he mean to you? Did he beat you?"

"Oh, no! My father was very good to me. And he always brought me presents back from Montreal."

They sat there for the next hour or more exchanging pieces of their personal history, although Charlie remembered nothing of his life before he came to the Mission School. To him, it seemed like his life had started over when Captain Gordon took him in, and his new life had been quite overwhelming at first. Now his best friend was telling him of his family life that had somehow been taken away. It all seemed so unfair.


"I must go now, mom ami," Dominic said. "I must prepare for a journey."

"Journey? "Where are you going?" Charlie asked.

"Down the big river to my uncle's village."

"Are you gonna go live with them? Aren't you coming

back?" There was worried concern in Charlie's voice, as if he feared losing his friend.

"No, I am not going to live with them. I will return after three days. I have to tend the cows."

"When are you going?"

"Next Friday evening, when I bring the cows back from pasture."

"Can I go with you?" Charlie asked eagerly.

"It will be a long hard journey," Dominic said, trying to discourage Charlie. But then it occurred to him that maybe a companion on such a voyage would be to his advantage. "Have you ever paddled a canoe?"

"No," Charlie replied. "But I can learn."

# Chapter 24

*I*t wasn't easy convincing Maria that this was to be just a simple fishing excursion that would last three or four days. Charlie was a bit on edge not telling her the entire truth, but he couldn't see that any harm would come of it. "We'll be home again before the captain returns, and I'll be with an expert boatman and fisherman who is going to show me all the good fishing spots. We'll camp in safe places at night and cook the fish we catch during the day and..."

"All right!" Maria finally gave in after hours of pestering from the boy. She thought that perhaps she was making a mistake, but Charlie seemed so enthusiastic about this adventure, and it would be healthy for him to spend some recreational time with someone near his own age. He *had* been quite obedient, and he hadn't been into any mischief lately. And she could use a few days to herself.

"All right," she said again calmly after a brief deliberation. "I'll pack a suitcase for you. You'll need plenty of clean shirts and trousers and—"

"No, Maria," the boy protested. "I'll find the things I need myself. We're camping, and we're traveling light. There won't be any formal dinner parties, so I don't need a suitcase full of clothes."

"Are you sure?"

"Quite."

For the next few days the two boys met on the La Crosse River bank, fished, swam, and occasionally planned their trip down the Mississippi. Since Dominic was the more experienced in such matters, Charlie simply followed his guidance. "We'll take only the things we need: blankets, a hatchet to cut firewood, and our fishing poles and tackle."

"What about food?" Charlie asked.

"We can bring some, but mostly we'll eat the fish we catch."

Charlie was so excited about this new adventure he could hardly fall asleep at night, but finally the day came for their planned departure. So anxious to get started, he carried his bundle of blankets and one change of clothes, the basket of food that Helen had prepared for him, and his fishing pole and tackle to the riverbank more than two hours before Dominic was to arrive. That gave him plenty of time to dig an ample supply of earth worms.

The sun was sinking low in the western sky when Dominic came up the little river. Charlie just gawked at his beautiful canoe; he had never seen such a fine one as this.

"My father gave it to me," Dominic said. "When my uncle taught me how to paddle a canoe alone, my father thought I should have one of my own, and he brought this back from Montreal. He said it would be stronger and safer for me than the Indian canoes."

And it was a fine canoe, made from light-weight but hard and strong wood, precisely hand-crafted by a French-Canadian boatswain, coated with layers of varnish that made it shine like a mirror. Henri Bouton had presented his youngest son with the craft as a gift upon returning from one of his numerous voyages to Montreal. It was one of a kind, and everyone who knew the boy, knew how much he treasured that boat.

They stowed Charlie's things in the canoe, and then Dominic instructed Charlie how to board the canoe, placing one foot carefully in the center when he stepped in, to avoid tipping the boat to one side. Once Charlie was on the front seat, Dominic showed him how to hold the paddle and how to pull strokes through the water. Then he climbed aboard onto the rear seat, and moments later they were gliding down the La Crosse River, headed for the Mississippi.

It didn't take Charlie long to get the feel of it, and by the time they had maneuvered around many bends and reached the Mississippi, the two were paddling in nearly perfect sync.

But by that time, too, the last golden rays of sunshine had given way to the gray curtain of dusk. As they paddled southward by the new Coleman Lumber Mill the shadows grew darker, and soon the lights of the town were left behind them. The farther downstream they drifted, less frequent were the faint glows of cabin lights, visible only moments, sometimes, because of the trees. The river wandered on through what seemed to Charlie a wild territory, especially in the dark, where loomed on either side the silhouettes of hills and bluffs towering over them like giant monsters. But he wasn't frightened by any of this; instead, he was quite intrigued.

"We'll stop to camp soon," Dominic said after they had gone downriver about four miles.

"How will we ever find a place? It's so dark."

"Oh, *mon ami*," replied Dominic. "Don't you remember? I know all the good places on the river... even in the dark."

A short while later they beached the canoe on a sandy strip. Beyond the sand Charlie could barely make out the dark outline of trees.

"This is an island," Dominic explained. "I've been here many times. It's a good place to camp for the night."

"How big is the island?" Charlie asked.

"Oh, big enough to be safe, and small enough so there aren't any wild animals that live here."

"Wild animals?"

"*Oui, mon ami.* None that will bother us or steal our food."

They drug the canoe far out of the water up onto the beach and then went in search of some dry firewood among the trees. Within a short while, Dominic had a crackling campfire that lit up the beach and a small open area in the trees where they unrolled their blankets.

They sat by the fire and ate bread and cheese and pieces of cold chicken from Charlie's basket and drank milk from the jug that Dominic had just received from Mr. Kellogg at the hotel that afternoon. Dominic seemed quiet—more than usual—as if something troubled him.

"Is something wrong?" Charlie asked. "Am I not good enough at paddling the canoe?"

"Oh, *pas du tout*... you do just fine, *mon ami*. I am very tired. We should go to sleep now," Dominic said, changing the subject. "Tomorrow morning we will catch fish for our breakfast."

"When will we get to your uncle's village?"

"Tomorrow afternoon. It's still a long way."

They snuggled into their blankets. Charlie watched the fire until it slowly diminished to a bed of hot red coals. He could hear Dominic's slow, steady breathing in the stillness of the night, and he knew he was asleep. But Charlie wasn't all that sleepy, so he lay there gazing up at the stars and listened to an owl hooting somewhere, and another answering it from somewhere else. Moonlight washed over everything and it made the ripples on the river sparkle.

# *Chapter 25*

*C*harlie wasn't so accustomed to this type of accommodations, so he drifted in and out of periods of sleep. He didn't know how long he had slept when he awoke and noticed that a tree—a tall poplar—seemed more distinct than any trees had appeared all night, and then more trees revealed their silvery-green leafy details as the soft pearly dawn floated its first light over the river. Then he heard familiar early morning sounds: cher, cher, cher, cher... a blackbird, answered by another farther away.

Charlie sat up, stretched out his arms, yawned, and quickly pulled a blanket up around his shoulders again as it was just a little chilly.

"Bonjour, M'sieur Charlie." His stirring had awakened Dominic.

Charlie giggled at the French greeting. "Good morning to you, too," he replied.

*"Sacre bleu! Merveilleux!"* Dominic said in a loud

whisper.

Charlie watched the hills across the water come out of their shadows. "I'm not sure what you just said, but I think it means 'What a wonderful morning.' Is that about right?"

Dominic grinned. "That's close enough."

The glorious morning showered down silver pencils of sunlight through the overhanging tree boughs, and the warm glow gradually spread over the woods and the wild landscape; the river sparkled and danced.

From beyond a bend in the river came the familiar whistle of a steamboat. The sound echoed between the hills, and the boys craned their necks to look upriver. First to appear were the four red-shirted oarsmen at the front of the log raft, pushing on the ends of their long oars or "sweeps" that pivoted on yokes mounted at the very front of the raft, steering the raft around the river bend. Eight hundred feet behind them, the steamboat appeared, pushing the huge mass of logs downstream. Dominic jumped up and waved jubilantly; a few arms aboard the *Nellie Thomas* waved back and the pilot sounded a little toot from the whistle, but the oarsmen at the front of the raft were too busy guiding the raft to even notice him waving on the island.

The two boys watched in awe until the raft and stern-wheeler were out of sight. "Someday," Charlie said, "I'm gonna work on a boat like that."

Dominic jerked his head to look at Charlie, a little surprised. He had never heard Charlie mention any interest in riverboats before. "Me too," he said, after a fleeting thought that it might be better than farming raced through his head. "Maybe we can work together on the same boat."

Just then another steam whistle sounded from downstream, and the *Nellie Thomas'* whistle answered it, just like the owls and blackbirds had done, Charlie thought. A few minutes later, the *Phil Sheridan*, the fastest packet boat on the Mississippi steamed by on its way upriver to La Crosse. Charlie joined in with the waving this time that resulted in another whistle blast and a few hearty waves from the pilot house. And then it was gone around the bend.

"Let's catch some fish for breakfast," Dominic suggested.

After a good meal of sunfish they caught on the other side of the island, they sat on their little beach for a while and watched a couple more raft boats pass by.

"How did you learn to cook fish so good?" Charlie asked.

"I started helping my mother in the kitchen when I was very young. When she got sick and died, I just kept on cooking for our family."

"Well, you sure are good at it."

Dominic shrugged his shoulders. His gaze seemed to be searching for some far-away place, and Charlie thought he might be intruding if he asked any more questions. So he just sat there, shoulder to shoulder with Dominic, watching the river.

It was mid-morning when they packed their gear in the canoe and paddled southward. Charlie watched mile after mile of river valley slide by. They had crossed over to the west shore line, and once they left the little town of Brownsville behind, there was nothing but open prairies, hills and trees. Charlie was so intrigued by all this new and unfamiliar scenery that he didn't realize his hunger until Dominic suggested they should stop and catch some fish for their lunch.

A few trees close to the bank provided a little shade while the boys dropped their lines in the water. They had each caught one small fish and were hoping for something better when an older man rowed past in a shabby-looking canoe. He wore dirty, tattered clothing, a scraggy black beard, and an unpleasant scowl. Charlie waved, trying to be polite and friendly, but the man only nodded and never raised a hand. He kept staring their way until he was well past them, and then he turned the small craft toward the bank and disappeared behind a point.

"I think there's a little stream that comes out there," said Dominic.

"He didn't look too friendly," replied Charlie.

"Prob'ly some old hermit that lives back in the hills."

No sooner than Dominic had spoken, the shabby canoe reappeared and the rough-looking character paddled out into the Mississippi again, headed upriver past the boys, and disappeared around the bend. Gone long enough for the boys to forget about him while they pulled in a few more fish—enough for their meal—the man didn't come by again until Dominic was preparing the fish for cooking and Charlie was tending a small fire.

"That's a mighty fine boat y' got there." The gruff voice startled Dominic. He hadn't noticed the rather stealth approach by the stranger.

"Bonjour, M'sieur," he answered. "Oui, it is a very fine bateau," he said to the man who was still in his canoe nosed up to the bank.

The man stared at the superb craftsmanship with envy

in his eyes. "Would ya sell this fine boat?" he asked, never lifting his eyes from it.

"No," Dominic cried. "My bateau is not for sale."

"I'll give ya fair price—"

"No, no, NO!" Dominic repeated. "It is not for sale at any price." His voice growled with anger.

The stranger seemed to understand that his request was not a welcomed one. Now, both boys stood shoulder to shoulder staring at him, suggesting that they no longer had any desire to continue the conversation. He pushed his canoe away from the bank with his paddle and rapidly maneuvered the craft back to the creek outlet where he had disappeared the first time.

# Chapter 26

*T*he boys finished their meal and continued on down the river. A couple of hours later, under a hot mid-afternoon sun, Dominic recognized the little inlet that was near the Indian village. His heart raced as they beached the canoe and jumped ashore. This was his mother's homeland, and soon he would see his uncle and cousins, and soon he would seek the answers to questions that had plagued him for so long. But something didn't seem right. The well-worn path from the river inlet to the village in the woods was covered with undisturbed grass and weeds. It looked as though it had not been traveled upon in quite some time. Quiet loneliness drifted on a soft breeze as Dominic led the way up the trail. But when they reached the place that should have been the edge of the village, there was nothing but trees and tall grass and wildflowers. There were no Indian lodges. There were no Indian children playing and running about. There were no steaming pots hanging over cooking fires. There were no Indian women weaving baskets. No fields of corn or squash. No barking dogs. Nothing.

Charlie was quick to figure out that this had been

Dominic's destination, even though the Indian boy said nothing. He could see the devastating disappointment in Dominic's eyes, and then waves of something awkward and unspoken passed between them.

Dominic sat down on a fallen tree trunk and gazed about the lost village. "My uncle's lodge was right over there," he said and pointed. "And my grandfather, the chief, lived there." He pointed to another spot.

Charlie sat beside him. "Your grandfather was the chief?"

"Oui."

"Where do you think they went?" Charlie asked.

"I do not know," Dominic replied. With elbows on knees, he buried his face in his hands.

Charlie laid a sympathetic arm across his friend's shoulders. He knew what it felt like to be alone, without family, and he wanted to do anything he could to help Dominic.

After a few long moments, Dominic straightened up again and stared sadly into Charlie's eyes. "I came here to seek advice from my uncle, but now I may never know the answers to my questions."

"What advice? What questions?"

"It all started a long time ago, before I was born," Dominic began to explain. "My mother still lived here in the village, and there was another Winnebago boy—he is a grown man now—who wanted to marry her. But my mother did not like him, did not want him for a husband."

"So... what happened?" Charlie asked.

"My father's first wife was drowned in the river during a spring flood. That next winter, he asked Morning Star— my mother—to stay on Barron's Island to help him care for his two little sons. The chief—my grandfather—gave his permission, because he and his people were grateful to the great French trader who provided so many good things for them. And when my father and Morning Star fell in love, the chief couldn't deny their marriage. That would ensure a strong relationship with the trader.

"Then I was born, and I was raised in French tradition, just as my older half-brothers. But my Indian uncles and cousins taught me how to fish and hunt, and swim and paddle a canoe."

"Well, what does that have to do with you coming here?" asked Charlie.

"Two summers ago, while the people from this village were at Barron's Island for the trading festival, the Winnebago man who wanted to marry my mother put a dark curse on my father."

"What?"

"Fighting Bear came to our house late one night. I saw him at our window looking in. And long after everyone else was asleep, I heard him outside, dancing and drumming and chanting, 'round and 'round the house."

"A dark curse?"

"Oui. You see, mon ami," Dominic explained. "Fighting Bear never saw a vision from the Great Spirit. Instead, he was entered into the circle of dark magic."

Charlie stared at his friend, puzzled.

"I know you do not understand the Indian customs and traditions, and that's why all this seems confusing to you."

"Yes, it *is* a bit confusing," Charlie said.

Dominic tried to clear up the confusion by telling Charlie about the rite of passage from boy to man in the Indian culture. "When and Indian boy reaches the age of manhood, he goes alone out into the wilderness with nothing. He fasts and becomes one with nature, and then in a dream while he sleeps, a vision comes to him from the Great Spirit, and he is given his own guiding spirit that will help protect him through all his days on earth."

"And Fighting Bear didn't see his vision?"

"No. Somehow, the dark spirits gained control of him, and he started performing his dark magic, and all the people of the village became afraid of him."

"So... how could your uncle help?"

"He's the only one who could talk to Fighting Bear... find out about the curse... find out what has happened to my father."

"But maybe nothing has happened to your father," Charlie said. "You were in the house, too, and nothing has happened to you." Then he looked down at the little leather pouch hanging at Dominic's chest and he laid his hand upon it. "Oh, yeah... this is protecting you, right?"

"You learn fast, mon ami."

"Well, it's plain to see that they don't live here anymore," said Charlie, consoling his friend. "Should we go looking for them?"

"Where are you going to look, mon ami? We don't know which direction to start."

Charlie rubbed his chin and stared at the ground, thinking a few moments. "I guess you're right."

"Oui, mon ami. We could spend weeks searching."

Charlie gazed around the site where once had been a village of people. The forest and surrounding hills seemed to hold this spot in a comforting embrace. It was easy to see why they had chosen this location for their village, and he wondered why they would have left such a beautiful place. "So... what should we do now?" he asked.

"There is only one thing to do," replied Dominic. "Start back up the river. We'll find a place to camp for the night."

Charlie soon discovered that paddling the canoe upstream required a little more effort than he had experienced on the trip down with the current. "We must stay close to the banks," said Dominic. "The current isn't so strong there."

They had traveled up the river, waving to the passing steamboats with their rafts of logs and lumber. The crews always returned the greeting, and some called out "Frenchy!" when they recognized the boy and his canoe. Some of the pilots even tooted the steam whistle.

# *Chapter 27*

*T*hey were nearly as far as they had come down that afternoon when they spotted a suitable campsite on the west bank where a grove of scrub oak nearly met the water's edge. The bank sloped down from a level plateau that looked as though it had been put there just for them. It seemed quite solitary, and there was a good supply of dry wood for a campfire.

That night, after they had caught fish and eaten their supper, they sat next to the campfire while Dominic told Charlie more about his Indian relatives and how his father was ashamed that he had a son with dark skin. "He was a proud French gentleman," Dominic explained. "He knew a lot of important people in Montreal, and he once said that he would never take me there with him. I would embarrass him."

"So... he didn't love you?"

"Oh, yes, mon ami. He loved me very much. He took good care of me, just like my half-brothers. And he always brought me presents—nice presents—from Montreal." The boy pointed to the canoe that was just barely visible in the light from the fire. "My canoe... he gave me that canoe. He wanted me to have the very best canoe so I would be safe on the water."

Charlie agreed that it was the nicest canoe he had ever seen.

Then Dominic retrieved the polished wooden tackle

box and held it for Charlie to see. "This is the last present he gave me," he said as he opened the lid. Charlie felt almost envious because all he had to compare was a rusty tin can.

Then Dominic brought out another wooden box and removed the flute. "My brother Jacques gave me this."

"Can you play it?" Charlie asked.

Dominic just grinned and began playing a lively tune that suggested dancing. And dance he did, around the campfire, and then Charlie joined him, mocking Dominic's steps, clapping and cheering. It was great fun.

The crisp sound of the flute sailed out over the river and echoed among the hills. Charlie was amazed at his friend's musical talent, and he was glad to see Dominic's spirit lifted from his earlier depression.

"Wow!" Charlie said when they sat by the fire again. "How did you learn to play so good?"

"My uncle made me a flute from a willow branch when I was little and my mother taught me a few Indian songs. The rest I have taught myself."

Ever since Charlie had made acquaintance with Dominic he had admired him. But now, he felt even a stronger friendship building between them. He realized what a wonderful person Dominic was, and that it seemed so unfair that he had been left so alone. He was sure, too, that the Indian boy felt more confidence in their friendship, because he seemed more comfortable in talking about himself and his family than he ever had before.

"You're lucky, y' know," Charlie said.

"What do you mean, mon ami?"

"You're lucky that you have a family to remember. I don't have that. I don't remember my real family at all."

139

Dominic stared questioningly.

"I lived at the Mission School nearly all my life. They told me that I was brought there by a man they thought was my father, but they weren't really sure. He died there that same night. They said I cried, but I don't remember any of it."

"Nothing at all?"

"Nothing."

"But you are not sad about it?"

"It's hard to be sad about something you never had."

They talked for a while longer, and then decided they should try to get some sleep. They had a long day's journey ahead.

# Chapter 28

$C$harlie had slept quite soundly through his second night in the open air, and he awoke startled as Dominic shook his shoulder. "Wake up, mon ami! Wake up! The canoe is gone!"

"Canoe? Gone?" Charlie rubbed his eyes and squinted in the early morning sun.

"Oui. My bateau! *MON DIEU!* It is gone!" Dominic cried.

Charlie sprang to his feet and they both ran down to the riverbank where the canoe had been.

"It couldn't have just floated away," Dominic said. "It was completely out of the water."

"And you didn't get up during the night and—"

"No, no... I didn't wake up all night. Mon dieu! How can this be?" He fell to his knees and bowed his head in despair.

"Well, someone must've taken it," Charlie said as he

gazed up and down the river. He couldn't see very far in either direction because of trees and the river's bends. But a thought suddenly came to him. "That man that we saw yesterday. He sure seemed like he wanted your canoe awful bad," he said.

Dominic lifted his head and opened his eyes wide. "You're right. He probably saw us come here... and then he came to steal it when we were asleep."

"That would be my guess," Charlie added. "That creek we saw him go to isn't far from here, is it?"

"Not far at all. And that's where we'll find my canoe."

"But how will we get it back?" Charlie asked. "He certainly didn't look like the kind of chap that would just give it back."

"Then we will have to just take it... like he took it from us. But first, we must hide our things. We'll come back for them after we get the bateau."

They packed up all their belongings, hid the bundles under some blackberry bushes, and then set out along the riverbank to find the creek. They hadn't gone far when they realized that even paddling upstream against the current was much easier work than getting through the brush, and sometimes wading across swampy inlets and ditches. Their progress was slow and the sun very hot. After more than an hour of fighting their way through the thickets, their further passage was stopped by a muddy inlet partially hidden by reeds, and not more than fifty yards upstream they could see the grassy bank where they had fished the day before.

"This is it," Dominic said quietly as he crouched and gazed around curiously. He seized Charlie's arm and pulled him down, too, to make sure they were both well concealed in the tall weeds.

"The bateau is up there," Dominic whispered, pointing up the stream. He could see a thin column of smoke rising that appeared to be about a hundred yards away. "We need to be very quiet now."

They crept on cautiously, following the creek away from the river until they saw the source of the smoke. Up ahead on the opposite side was a low cabin, just as shabby-looking as the canoe the man had the day before. They had come upon the man's dwelling, but there was no one in sight.

"Where d'ya think he is?" Charlie whispered.

"Perhaps inside the cabin... there is smoke coming from the chimney... he's cooking."

Not far from the cabin, the creek widened to a large pool, a portion of which was occupied by a green new growth of cattails. The old shabby canoe was tied to a post driven into the bank, but the boys could not see Dominic's canoe.

"It must be there somewhere," Dominic whispered.

They continued to sneak closer, watching carefully for the appearance of their enemy.

"Look, there," Charlie said and pointed. Just barely visible he saw what he thought was the shiny wooden hull of Dominic's canoe, mostly concealed by the cattails around it. The man had definitely tried to hide it.

"How are we gonna get it?" Charlie asked. "It's so close to his house."

"I will swim to it," Dominic replied. "You go back downstream. Find a place where you can get close to the water... where we can get into the canoe. I will bring it down and then we can paddle quickly back out to the river."

Dominic took off his clothes and handed them to Charlie. Charlie watched as he slipped silently into the water. When he reached the large pool, Dominic disappeared under the surface.

Charlie watched and worried, but in a short while, Dominic's head popped up near the cattails. He looked around in all directions to see that he had not been detected by the enemy. Then he motioned to Charlie, urging him to go downstream where he would be out of sight.

Charlie didn't want to just leave his friend alone, but he also knew that for the plan to work, he had to be ready to board the canoe quickly, so he turned and hastily backtracked along the creek, confident that the Indian boy would be successful.

Dominic took hold of his canoe and slowly, quietly, inched it out from the cattail bed, raised up high enough to see that both the paddles were still inside, and immediately submerged again, with the canoe between him and the cabin. Without making a single splashing noise, he propelled himself across the pool holding the craft with one hand, and continued downstream until he was out of sight from the cabin.

The creek was much shallower here, forcing Dominic to wade instead of swim, and that made more noise. He hoped Charlie was near.

Charlie *was* near, waiting just around the next bend of the crooked stream. He tossed the clothes into the canoe; they both climbed aboard, and started paddling. But as they got closer to the Mississippi, the creek became too shallow. With two people in the canoe, it drug on the bottom and they could go no farther.

"We'll have to get out... wade the rest of the way," Dominic said.

They both got out and sloshed through the shallow water, pulling the canoe along.

"HEY! You come back here, you thief!" the gruff voice called out from up on the bank. "You stole my canoe!" the man yelled angrily.

The boys turned to look, startled. There was the man stumbling along the bank through the weeds, but keeping pace with them.

"This is not your canoe!" Dominic cried out. "You stole it from us."

But the filthy-clothed stranger kept yelling and cursing. "I'll drown you both in the river when I catch you... you good-for-nothin' thievin' scoundrels!" Then he jumped into the water and came after the boys, splashing through the shallow water, his long legs taking bigger strides than the boys could manage while maneuvering the canoe. He soon caught up to them, grabbed the stern point of the canoe with one hand and Dominic's arm with the other. He stood two heads taller than either of them, and his grip on Dominic's arm was firm and hurtful.

"Let go of me!" yelled the boy, pounding on the man's clenched grip with little effect.

"Let go of my canoe, you little thief!" the mangy character returned.

"It's NOT your canoe!" Dominic repeated.

Out of pure instinct, Charlie scooped up his paddle from inside the craft. The man was so occupied with the struggle from Dominic that he didn't notice Charlie's action, and he didn't see it coming. But Dominic did. He ducked as Charlie swung the paddle with all his might, and—WHAP—the flat end of the paddle struck the side of the man's head, sending him reeling backwards, falling and splashing into the water near the bank.  The boys didn't wait to see if he would get up again.  When they saw his head wobble a few times and one hand come up to it, they both grabbed the canoe and pushed it as fast as they could muster, splashing their way to the opening with its fringe of reeds, out into the Mississippi and deeper water.  When they hopped into the canoe they could hear the nasty oaths the man was yelling at them, promising to kill them if he caught them.

By the time they reached their campsite, the sun had dried off Dominic.  He gathered his clothes, hopped ashore, and quickly dressed.  "Get our bundles out of the bushes, mon ami," he told Charlie.  "Let's get started up the river before that wild man comes after us again."

They were at least thirty yards out into the river when they passed the mouth of the stream where they had had the close encounter.  As they paddled by, they saw the man, wild with rage, in his wretched old canoe.  "There, you see?" Charlie said.  "He's gotten his canoe and he's coming after us again!"

"Paddle fast, mon ami... *à tout vitesse!*"

But they were too far away from the bank, out in the river channel where the current was strong, and making forward progress was difficult and slow.  Charlie's arms ached, but he was determined to paddle as long as it took to get away from the crazy man.  He glanced over his shoulder, only to see that the man was making faster headway closer to the shore where the current was less.  "He's getting closer," Charlie whispered hoarsely.

"Oui, I'm afraid so," replied Dominic.

It was clear to see that the man intended to get ahead of them and then come at them with the current to his advantage. And within a short time, that's exactly what he did.

But there was soon to be another factor that the man did not expect, nor did Charlie. "Turn out and paddle toward the main channel," Dominic said in a loud whisper. "Head right in front of that steamboat coming upstream." Apparently, he was the only one who had noticed it coming.

Charlie looked back. "What? We'll get run over! We'll be killed!"

"No, no, mon ami. Just do it!"

# Chapter 29

*C*harlie followed the instructions and turned the canoe out into the path of the oncoming steamer. He thought he was committing suicide, but when he looked back at the savage man in the other canoe who was about to overtake them, he began to paddle faster. But it was already too late. The man had much more momentum built up coming at them downstream. He managed to get close enough to grab the side of the boys' canoe and held up his paddle in such a way as to ward off the attempts Charlie and Dominic made to beat him away.

Dominic's cries for help were well-received aboard the steamer. She chugged slowly right alongside where the struggle was taking place and then the huge paddlewheel reversed and the big boat stopped. The rafter *Union* was on her way home after delivering a raft of lumber to DuBuque, and the French boy was no stranger to her crew.

Crewmen on the steamer were yelling at the man before he realized that they were not there to aid him. He just kept cursing and snarling. "These varmints stole my canoe! I'll have their hide, I will!"

The close proximity of the steamer turned Charlie's blood cold, especially when the canoe bumped into the hull. He didn't realize the steamer was completely stopped as he had been so occupied with defending himself and Dominic against the onslaught of their vicious pursuer.

"Frenchy!" Charlie heard one of the crewmen call out. "What have you gotten yourself into this time?"

The strange man in the old canoe growled again: "They stole my boat and I want it back."

Just then Captain Anderson appeared at the steamer's gunwale, and Charlie came to realize that the men on the big boat were there to help them. "You'd better back off, old man," said one of the crew, "or I'll poke a hole in your boat and you can swim or drown... I won't much care."

"But that's my boat. They took it, and I want it back."

Captain Anderson stepped forward. "You are a liar, mister. I happen to *know* this boy, and I also happen to know that *this is his canoe.* I should take you aboard and have you arrested for molesting these boys. Now paddle your sorry behind out of here or I'll *personally* sink that tub of yours."

All the time the captain was reprimanding the man, a couple of crewmen pulled Charlie and Dominic on board the big boat, and two more hoisted the beautiful canoe up onto the deck.

"FULL SPEED AHEAD!" shouted the captain. The pilot

blasted the whistle a couple of times, and the boiling sound of the paddlewheel churning the water accompanied the hiss of steam escaping from the engine vents. Charlie watched in awe as the boat slowly pulled away from the man in the shabby canoe, sitting there like a whipped pup, knowing he had been defeated.

"Now, Frenchy," the captain said. "What on earth are you doing all the way down here?"

"Fishing, M'sieur Captain Anderson," Dominic replied. "And this is Charlie, *un ami à moi.*"

"A friend of yours, eh?" said the captain. "And why was that nasty old man chasing you?"

"He stole my bateau while we slept last night, and we found where he lived and..."

Dominic told the whole story to the captain while Charlie just stood by and listened. It was clear to him that the captain and all the crew members knew Dominic by the way they greeted each other. And it was clear that Dominic didn't want them to know that the real reason he had come here was to visit an Indian village—his *relative's* village.

"Well, you're safe now," said Captain Anderson. "And we'll have you boys back home in a couple of hours." He put a hand on each of their shoulders and guided them to the stairway to the upper deck. "You boys hungry?"

"Oui, M'sieur. That man kept us from having our breakfast this morning."

"Well I'm sure Cookie can find something for you."

*"Merci, M'sieur."*

"You are quite welcome, Frenchy."

While they wolfed down stacks of pancakes with maple syrup and butter, Charlie's curiosity got the best of him. "You know all these guys?" he said in a low tone.

"Oui, mon ami. They are all my friends. I know almost everybody at the boat yard."

"They all call you *Frenchy*."

"Oui. That is the only name they ever call me." Dominic stared seriously into Charlie's eyes. "And you should, too."

From that day forward, *Frenchy* was the only name Charlie ever called his friend.

# Chapter 30
## Early Spring: 1882

*C*harlie Martin was starting his second season as a deckhand aboard Captain Gordon's log raft boat. After another year or two of learning the workings of the vessel and understanding the function of every crew member, he would advance to the pilothouse as a cub pilot, and perhaps someday he would wear a captain's hat. That had been Captain Gordon's intensions from the very start—to nurture his legacy—so there would be another Captain Gordon to follow in his footsteps as a Mississippi River pilot.

Now Gordon was Captain of a relatively new boat in the McDonald fleet, the *Bella Mac*, a powerful stern-wheeler that was as good as any rafter on the Upper Mississippi. He had hand-picked his officers to work with him, and he was supremely happy to have his best friend, Frank McIntyre as his second pilot.

Charlie and Frenchy weren't spending so much time together now, as Charlie's life was aboard a steamboat most of the spring, summer, and autumn, and although their friendship had grown stronger, there wasn't much more than a day now and then for fishing and swimming and canoeing. Frenchy spent enough time around the boatyard, though, to know when the big boats would arrive and depart, and he was always there to welcome

*Bella Mac's* crew home after a river journey, as he did with many other crews. He wasn't that cute little boy anymore, but instead he was growing into a handsome young man. But he had never lost his charming, boyish personality, and one would be hard-pressed to find anybody who didn't still adore Frenchy. He made the rounds to greet all the crewmen, and for his best friend, Charlie Martin, the customary French hug was secretively a little more meaningful.

Over the years, Charlie had never divulged the secret of Frenchy's Indian heritage, and for that Frenchy was grateful. It was one of the elements that strengthened the bond between them. But sometimes it was difficult to hide their friendship, always sneaking off to some remote rendezvous to fish and swim and explore the unexplored. And when it became well-known that they were close pals, no one appeared to be concerned for the adopted son of gentleman Captain Gordon. It seemed quite natural that two boys nearly the same age would share so many common interests.

Captain Gordon would have taken a more keen interest in Frenchy, too, had it not been for the boy dressed in peasant's clothing. He didn't realize that the boy was born of aristocratic blood, or that his father was from the upper-class merchants of Montreal. He had never listened to Frenchy talk—other than the usual greetings from time to time—to recognize his speech as being impeccably correct, rarely using slang or inappropriate words. What he did hear was the boy often using French words and phrases; that tended to mask the boy's cultural refinement.

He had been rather displeased with Charlie when he learned that Captain Anderson had rescued the two boys from that madman so far downriver, but he was more upset with Maria for consenting to the departure in the first place. Charlie's punishment had been spending a week helping James with work in the garden and other chores, including putting a fresh coat of paint on the carriage house. No fishing or swimming was allowed the entire week. It proved to be a long week for Charlie.

Now it was early March, and there was always plenty of excitement in the air at this time of year among all the men who made their living on the river. Boats were being readied for when the ice was out and the first log rafts could be taken downriver on the high water. Mills farther south where they didn't have readily available the great pine forests of the north were eagerly awaiting a new supply of logs, so their silent saw blades could once again sing after a long winter.

Captain Gordon was no exception when it came to excitement for the new shipping season, and Charlie, too, had certainly learned to love the river and the life of a river man. He and the captain were spending their days at the boatyard, getting the *Bella Mac* ready for her first trip of the season.

One evening Helen was busy in the kitchen preparing the family supper when she heard a knock at the door. It was a messenger delivering a letter addressed to Captain Gordon, and it was marked *URGENT*. Helen took the letter right to Mr. Gordon in the den where he and Maria and Charlie were relaxing and having coffee. Gordon opened the letter, read, and then handed it to Maria. She studied the paper and frowned.

"What is it?" asked Charlie.

"A letter from Mr. Stanley at the Mission School," said Maria. She stared at her father sadly. "We must..."

"I don't see any harm in it," Gordon said, and he turned to Charlie. "Do you remember Mrs. Champlain at the school?"

"Oh... yes," Charlie replied with a smile. He had fond memories of the old woman who had so kindly cared for him when he was little and helpless. "She was so good to me... and I've never been back to visit her."

"Well, that's mostly my fault, my boy," said Gordon. "It seems that she is in very poor health... maybe dying. Apparently she has requested several times to see you."

Charlie approached the captain's side. "May I go see her?" he asked.

"Of course you may. We'll go and see her right now."


Charlie didn't encounter very many familiar faces at the school—it had been several years since he last saw anyone there. But Mr. Stanley hadn't changed much, although he seemed quite pleased with Charlie, whom he had expected to return to the school a short time after he left. He secretly admitted—if only to himself—that he had underestimated Charlie's qualities, and certainly Mr. Gordon's tolerance and determination. "I'm proud of you, Jules," he said as he shook the boy's hand.

"My name is Charlie Martin, now," the boy replied. He wanted to say *you weren't proud of me five years ago,* but good manners stopped him.

"Well, Mrs. Champlain knew you as her little Jules. She is quite ill, and sadly, the doctor says she is likely to die soon. But lately she has spoken of you often and repeatedly asked to see you again. You were very special to her, and I'm so glad—for her sake—that you're here."

They walked solemnly to the infirmary where the old nurse lay comfortably. Her eyes lit up when Charlie approached; though he had grown and matured since they were last together, she recognized him and she held out a feeble hand, urging him to sit down beside her.

The boy obliged, still holding her hand.

"And you've grown to such a fine lad," she said, but her voice was frail and weak, and it was clear that even speaking was difficult for her.

Charlie gently squeezed her hand, smiled warmly, and leaned down to place a kiss on her cheek. No words were necessary to explain the special place he had for Mrs. Champlain in his heart. She had been like a mother to him —the only mother he could remember. And now, his actions were as if he had answered the most important wish of the old woman's entire life.

She had little more to say other than petitioning Charlie to promise another visit, and as he and Mr. Gordon were about to leave, her gaze shifted from the boy to Mr. Stanley. "The package," she said.

"Oh, yes," Stanley said, as if he had forgotten something. He crossed the room to a table, picked up a small bundle wrapped in brown paper and handed it to Charlie. "She wanted you to have this. She said she found these things in the old man's coat pocket after he died."

Charlie opened the package with Gordon and Stanley looking on. It contained a child's linen undergarment, plainly marked "Reginald Van Hugh III" and a colorful children's picture book, frayed and torn and creased through the center from being folded double to fit in a pocket. It was the familiar old story of *Little Red Riding Hood*, but the hand-written inscription on the cover in a delicate hand read:

*"For my darling Reggie on his second birthday,*
*Rita Van Hugh, Scranton, June 30 1866."*

Captain Gordon examined the name on the garment, and then the inscription on the book. "I thought you said the boy's father was a rough old tramp who died here in the infirmary."

"That's what we thought for many years," said Stanley. "Then Mrs. Champlain revealed these things just recently. She had kept them secretly all these years." He pushed Gordon and Charlie out the door and closed it behind him. "My guess is that she didn't want to lose this child, so she hid his real identity."

Gordon stuffed the garment and book in his pocket.

"I have sent several letters," Stanley added. "But so far, there have been no inquiries about the boy."

On the way home, Charlie asked, "Does this mean I'll have to change my name again?"

"I don't know, Charlie. Depends on whether or not any of your kinfolk show up. Do you *want* to change your name?"

"No! I want to be Charlie Martin, and I want you to be my father and Maria to be my sister. And I want to stay here and become a riverboat captain... just like you."

The captain put his arm around the boy. "And we'll try to keep it just that way, Charlie Martin."

# *Chapter 31*

*F*renchy wandered among the few stacks of freight on the levee. He gazed at the barges mounded with cordwood and coal that lay in the icy water at the landing. On summer evenings, this is where men sat watching the silent river, telling their river stories. Most of the ice was melted and gone from the Black River, but much of the stuff still floated down on the Mississippi channel, too much, yet, for the big boats to safely navigate. Frenchy knew, though, that there would soon be plenty of activity here. To this port came steamboats up from St. Louis and down from St. Paul. In earlier days, crowds would gather at the first sign of them—a cloud of smoke beyond the bend and the sound of a whistle—and they would remain until the boat came in, hissing and splashing, the pilot's bell clanging signals to the engineer, and the mate calling out orders to the deckhands. Then passengers paraded across the landing stage; freight was carted off and freight was carted on. All this while, the town was linked to far-away, unseen places, and when the boat departed, the world left with it, until the next whistle sounded.

But the excitement of a steamboat arrival drew smaller crowds now, if any at all. Arrivals were commonplace; the novelty had lost most of its brilliance and the railroads had dulled the glamour, stealing much of the passenger and freight business from the river. But one element remained: as soon as the ice was gone, out in the main channel would pass the big log rafts—acres of pine logs from the St. Croix and Chippewa River valleys. For the past decade steamboats had pushed the giant rafts downstream, and for thirty years before that log rafting had been a silent business, the huge slow islands floating on the current without a sound, only the cry of the steersman and the clatter of the cook's kettles. At night, the sounds of singing and frolicking by the red-shirted rafters around a small fire burning on a mound of sand in the middle of the raft could be heard moving slowly down the channel; it was their only entertainment during the long journeys, as the only time the rafts stopped until they reached their destination was when they were tied up at shore or island during storm or heavy fog.

The logs on which they rode came from the greatest pine forest in the world. The northern rivers—the Wisconsin, the Black, the Chippewa, the Red Cedar, the St. Croix—all flowed through the silence of the wilderness to the Mississippi amidst seemingly endless stands of tall pine, spruce and hemlock. And it was of this grand gift of nature that would build cities in the growing West. Everything was wood—barns, houses, shops, churches, fences, plank roads and board sidewalks, wagons, boat docks and steamboats. And it was the lumber industry that so many men's lives depended on. Frenchy realized now that this should his new destiny; that he should follow his heart onto a riverboat and learn the skills of rafting logs and lumber.

Captain Gordon and Charlie gazed around the Boat Store as they waited for Frank McIntyre, Louis, the captain's First Mate, and Bill, the cook, to join them. It was a busy place, buzzing with activity as stock boys emptied crates and filled the shelves and tables with fresh inventory getting ready for the new river season. Charlie had been there quite a few times last summer, when it had been one of his jobs to help "Cookie" carry the grocery boxes hack to the kitchen aboard the *Bella Mac*. He suspected he would be doing plenty of that again this year, too.

Located right on the levee, the Boat Store was operated by the McDonald Brothers. The basement consisted of ship supplies, rope, chain, pike poles, oars, and all the numerous articles used in steamboat operation. The upper or main floor carried a large stock of smoked and salted meats and groceries, usually of better grade than found in the normal grocery store. Packet boats usually wired the store from Lansing on the upstream trip, or from Winona on the trip down, requesting that fresh meat, fresh vegetables, and ice be obtained for them. They would pick up the other groceries from the store's regular stock.

On this day, though, Captain Gordon and his officers were there to make certain that supplies would be available in a few days when the *Bella Mac* would take the first raft of logs of the season down the Mississippi.

# *Chapter 32*
## Friday March 17, 1882

*F*rank McIntyre eased the 115-foot Bella Mac slowly alongside the 600-foot-long log raft that was tied up at the bank just below the McDonald's Black River boom. As the big boat inched along, Louis and his eight crewmen tossed the lines across the raft that would secure it into a manageable mass, and attach it to the tow boat. Charlie was right there helping and learning; Captain watched from the Texas deck. A couple of hours later the massive raft with four oarsmen at its bow coaxing it toward the main channel emerged from the mouth of the Black River. The first raft of the season was headed down the Mississippi.

The first raft to go downriver in the spring was a challenge as new sandbars could have formed changing the channel, and springtime floods were bound to have altered the banks and familiar landmarks that helped guide pilots on the river. But Captain Gordon and his second pilot, Frank McIntyre were up to the challenge. With this smaller raft, maneuvering new, unknown obstacles was less hazardous than with a full raft. Whenever there was nothing else for Charlie to do, he spent as much time as possible in the pilothouse learning from the masters.

So many changes, and yet the river had not changed—the mystery of midnight and the noon glare. Dawn and sunrise was always the same; first the stillness before the daybreak and then the stars blinked away with the approaching light; the black shorelines softened to gray and the river emerged from darkness under puffs of white fog. From the silent forest the first birds called and in the growing light the river reflected the gold and pink sky and the deep green of the tree-lined shores. Then the day suddenly and boldly marched in, and the world was full of sunlight.

And the river had moods: radiant in sunshine, majestic in moonlight, jeweled with the sparkling stars; mysterious in fog, and menacing under stormy skies. It changed with the seasons: frozen and motionless in January; high water in March, carrying fallen trees, fence rails, various pieces of timber, and the occasional skiff or canoe that had been left unsecured, too close to the river; low water in late summer exposing more rocks and sandbars and snags that did nothing but increase the hazards of navigation.

Fifty years earlier, the Upper Mississippi was a wilderness river. For nearly a thousand miles it flowed past forest, bluff and prairie. Then it had been the country of the Sauk, Winnebago, Chippewa and the Sioux, with Indian camps on the hills and Indian canoes and bull boats on the water. Not as frequent was a squatter's hut or a half-breed's shanty on the shore.

Near the mouth of the Wisconsin River the Bella Mac floated her raft past one of the oldest settlements in Wisconsin—Prairie du Chien—spred over a bench of land between the bold bluffs and the shining water. Until the railroad probed its way from Milwaukee to Prairie du Chien's riverbanks, it had been a drowsy place where the Indians brought their peltry to the French fur trading post. But now it had become an important commercial port. Farther south, on the Illinois side, a few miles up the Fever

River, what had started as a dozen huts and cabins clustered around a lead smelting furnace, was now the bustling city of Galena. On the west bank in Iowa, high on top of a hill, among the shallow pits of his lead mines, lay the grave of Julian Dubuque, overlooking the city named for him.

And that was as far as the Bella Mac would venture this trip. The logs were delivered and without delay, after all the towing gear was retrieved from the raft and the clerk, David McCannish had finished all the official business with the mill, Captain Gordon gave the order to turn the boat upstream and start the journey back to La Crosse.

Charlie, as well as most of the crew, enjoyed the return trips upriver. Because there was no raft to tend, it allowed a little more leisure time, especially for those manning the oars at the bow of the raft; that was hard work and a break was always welcomed.

The cooks, though, still had a busy schedule; everyone still had to eat. Charlie gave a hand in the galley sometimes so that young George McCannish, the cook's helper, could take a break. He was only twelve years old, and Charlie figured the only reason he had the job was because of his two older brothers, David, the Clerk, and William, one of the deckhands.

And sometimes Charlie would help out the firemen, Maurice and Dick, so they could have a little extra rest, too. Mostly, though, whenever possible, he spent his time in the pilothouse with Captain or Frank, learning navigation skills and how to read the river, and sometimes just to talk.

One evening after supper, while it was Gordon's watch at the wheel, Charlie stood beside him. "Cap'n," he said.

"I'm beginning to worry about Frenchy; his clothes seem a bit more shabby and ill-fitting now, and his spirit is drooping just a little."

"Oh?" the captain replied. He was well aware that the two boys were good friends, and although he had never given much consideration to Frenchy, he recognized Charlie's usual manner of caring for other people. He didn't know that Frenchy was wearing the last of the hand-me-down clothing left from his brothers; that the little money he earned during the summer was barely enough to buy food and supplies for the winter.

"I'd like to do something nice for him," Charlie continued. "He *is* my best friend, y' know... and he *did* save my life once. Well, *twice*, if you count the time we were picked up by Captain Anderson on the Union."

"What do you mean? Saved your life. What other time?" The captain tried not to sound alarmed.

"I never told you about it," Charlie said. "But I guess I can now." He hesitated a moment. "I fell in the La Crosse River once trying to get my fish line out of a tree branch. Frenchy pulled me out. And then he taught me how to swim."

"But Charlie," the captain said. "He's just a—"

"A wonderful person, and a real gentleman," the boy interrupted. "He's all alone, parents and brothers gone, has to take care of himself."

Gordon felt a little tickle in his throat. "Where does he live?"

"In a little log cabin on the island. But he can't buy clothes because he only makes enough money herding the cattle to buy food for the winter."

Moved by all this, Captain Gordon's interest grew with

Charlie's concern for his friend. "So, what do you want to do?"

"I've talked to some of the guys in the crew; they'd be willing to chip in a little, too. I'd like to bring Frenchy on a trip down the river with us as a guest; treat him to a haircut, and maybe a nice bath, and buy him some new clothes. He really is quite a gentleman, y' know."

The captain rubbed his chin, considering his son's gesture of generosity. "We'll be going to Clinton next trip."

"Could Frenchy come with us?"

"If you really want to do this... I don't see why not."

Charlie hugged the captain. "Thank you, Cap'n. And by the way... I think he'd like to work on a riverboat. He told me once."


When the Bella Mac pulled into her home port a couple of days later, Captain Gordon noticed from the pilothouse an exquisitely-dressed man waiting on the dock, and he appeared to be looking for this particular boat.

Frank McIntyre noticed him, too. "Now that fellow looks out of place as pants on a parakeet," he said to the captain. "Ain't no lumberman, that's for sure."

"I'll go down and see what he wants," Captain Gordon said. He casually ambled down the stairs to the main deck as Louis and his deckhands tied up the boat, and then he stepped across the wide gap between deck and dock as if it weren't even there.

Judging Gordon's attire, the stranger approached the captain. "Are you Captain Will Gordon?" he asked.

"I am."

The stranger offered his hand and they shook.

"My name is Samuel Henderson and I represent the

Van Hugh family of New York."

Gordon's smile slowly diminished when he heard mention of the Van Hugh *family*. In a moment he felt as though an anchor chain was wrapped around his heart and the anchor had just been tossed overboard. This could only mean that Charlie *had* a family, and if they had gone to the extent of sending a representative to find him, the chances of Charlie remaining in La Crosse were rather slim.

"We have received word from a Mr. Stanley," Henderson continued, "that you have in your custody a boy adopted from the orphanage."

The captain just listened. He knew what was coming.

"We have confirmed the boy's real name to be Reginald Van Hugh III. Is there someplace we might talk privately?"

Reluctantly, with great sadness in his voice, Gordon invited Mr. Henderson to his private quarters aboard the Bella Mac. When they were behind closed doors, Mr. Henderson presented his ploy.

"Reginald Van Hugh III is the son of Lieutenant Van Hugh II of the Union Army and his wife Rita. Lieutenant Van Hugh was killed during the Civil War. His wife fled to the West with their son. She settled in Winona, Minnesota where she soon fell ill and died."

"So the boy *is* truly an orphan," said Gordon.

Mr. Henderson barely acknowledged Gordon's statement and then went on. "Apparently, the little toddler wandered off while the mother was sick... or dying... and by the time she was found, the boy was gone, miles away, evidently picked up and carried off by some old tramp that happened to be passing by, uncaring of where the boy belonged. A thorough search of the immediate area where the boy disappeared was finally given up weeks later.

"It took some time to piece all this together, but by dates of the mother's death and the boy's arrival to the orphanage, he was with the old tramp for about three months traveling about the countryside where no one questioned the two of them together. It was the ferryboat operator at Read's Landing who remembered taking an old man and a child to Wisconsin, and a farmer and his wife who were on their way to market who had seen them along the river road, and they all said the ragged little boy clung to the old man affectionately. So naturally, it became nobody's business. And when the old man must've realized the condition of his own poor health, he took the boy to the orphanage."

"Charlie was too young," the captain said, "to explain where he came from or what had happened."

Mr. Henderson stared at Gordon questioningly. "Charlie?"

"Charles Martin Gordon. That's his name now."

"Oh, but I must tell you that the boy is heir to great fortune as *Reginald Van Hugh*, and my orders from the family are to return him to New York. He will be well cared for there by his relatives."

Gordon could feel tears forming. It was at that very moment that he came to realize that Charlie meant a great deal more to him than just a legacy to carry on the Gordon name amidst the Mississippi riverboats. He cared deeply for Charlie, and separating would be most difficult... for both of them.

# Chapter 33
## Friday March 24

*I*t was a dreamy sort of day as Frenchy watched the cows grazing contentedly. The swallows glided about in the gentle breeze that soothed his skin. The sky was pale blue above, scattered with mounds of shimmering clouds at the horizon. It seemed a day made for dreaming on the quiet slopes of pasture.

High above the city was a silvery cloud shaped like a feather, sleek and slender. Slowly it changed as the edges softened and spread until it had become a great wing. It reminded Frenchy of something that was just beyond the edge of his memory. Then he remembered what Gray Wolf had once said: "There are spirit signs in the clouds."

Could it be, even though he was only half Indian, that the spirits were guiding him? But what were they saying? For many long lazy minutes he watched the cloud as it drifted overhead and past the hills to the east, out of sight.

He leaned back against the big boulder and closed his eyes. He wondered about his future, now that it was quite certain his father and brothers would not return. He thought about his friendship with Charlie Martin: of all the friends he had made at the riverfront, his relationship with Charlie seemed to be the only one meaningful...

As if the very thought of Charlie had brought him up from the river, when he opened his eyes the boy was standing over him, grinning. Frenchy jumped up, catching hold of his friend's hands. Charlie was really there... not a dream.

"The men on the wharf told me I'd find you here."

Frenchy threw his arms around Charlie's shoulders. "Oui, mon ami! I'm so happy to see you again."

They sat in the shade of the big boulder; Frenchy saw the sadness suddenly appear in Charlie's eyes. "What is wrong, mon ami?"

Charlie nearly choked on the words: "A man from New York came to see us," he said.

Frenchy stared questioningly.

"Remember I told you that I lived at the Mission School most of my life?"

Frenchy nodded.

"Well, old Mrs. Chaplain who took care of me when I was little found some things with my real name... and my mother's name. But she kept it hidden until just now. And then Mr. Stanley sent some letters back east, to where my family is, I guess, and then this man showed up."

"Is he your real father?"

"No. According to him my real father was killed in the war."

"And your mother?"

"She brought me here when I was just a baby, but then she got sick and died. I don't remember any of it... I was too young.

"I guess I must've wandered off when my mother was sick. The old man found me and eventually took me to the Mission School by the time anyone realized I was missing. The neighbors searched for me, but they finally gave up, thinking I had either drowned in the river or was carried off by a wolf."

"So, what will happen now, mon ami?"

"The man from New York says I have to go back with

him and I have to live with some relatives who don't even know me."

"And so... you are leaving?"

Tears rolled down Charlie's cheeks. "That's just it, Frenchy. I don't want to start over with a new family. I have my family here, and I have you—my very best friend. I love this place and I love the river and the boats... and I love you and all the people in my life now. I'd rather die than leave this place with a stranger."

More tears streaked Charlie's face. He tried to wipe them away with his hand.

Frenchy moved close and put his arm across Charlie's shoulders. "I will miss you if you go away, mon ami. Oh, how I will miss you."

They sat in silence for a while, and then Charlie regained his composure. "Cap'n says I can go on one more trip down the river... and Frenchy, I want you to come with me, too."

Frenchy's eyes lit up. "Me? On the Bella Mac?"

"Yes, my friend. You. On the Bella Mac. And I'll have a surprise for you when we get to Clinton."

"What kind of surprise?"

"If I tell you now, it won't be a surprise."

"When will we go?"

"As soon as our lumber raft is ready... probably Monday or Tuesday, and we'll be gone for about two weeks."

Frenchy didn't have to give it much thought. "Okay. I will ask one of the other boys to tend the cows while I am away."

## Chapter 34
## Monday March 27

*U*nder any other circumstances, Captain Gordon would not have given that ragged, unkempt little man a second look. But Charlie loved him; and the crew adored him; and now the captain was about to find out why everyone admired this peasant of a boy. He only knew what Charlie had told him and tidbits from the other crewmen. Now he was helping to finance the boy's first trip down the Mississippi, and to fit him with some new clothing, all because he wanted to grant Charlie's wish—perhaps his last wish before he departed for New York to rejoin his family from which he had been lost for so long.

Frenchy had been on the boat with Charlie all night; he didn't want to be late, and Charlie was delighted that he was there. They would have to share a bunk for the entire trip; the Bella Mac was taking a full raft—six strings, 700 feet long and 270 feet wide—requiring a full crew, so all the crew's quarters were occupied.

At dawn, Louis and his men began preparing the raft—half logs and half lumber—while Charlie helped Bill and George tote the last boxes of groceries from the Boat Store. Frenchy insisted on helping with the task, too.

The captain stood in the pilothouse in the early morning light peering out the front windows, watching as the crew lashed the bow of the Bella Mac to the huge raft. She was pointed toward the mouth of the Black River, and soon she would be pushing the huge raft down the Mississippi. The log portion of the raft would be dropped off at Dubuque, and the lumber was destined for Clinton, Iowa, about five or six days away.

Gordon couldn't help but notice the enthusiasm bubbling from the boy he had seen so many times, but to whom he had never paid much attention. His smiling face was warmly received and greeted by every crewman as if they had been best friends for all time. Gordon was still curious to see why everyone liked this shabby-looking boy so much.

As the day wore on, Frenchy never seemed to tire of watching from the boiler deck the miles of river and forest solitude, marked by an occasional Indian mound or a lonely settler's cabin, shadowed by the towering bluffs. He marveled at the far forefront, 700 feet distant, where the oarsmen pulled on the long sweeps, steering the raft, bending it around to match the curves of the river, skillfully guiding it past sandbars and islands, and all the difficult places like Bad Axe Bend and Crooked Slough.

Captain Gordon was making his rounds of the boat late in the afternoon when he poked his head into the galley. Bill was his pride-and-joy cook, as really good cooks were rare, and Bill was one of the best on the river. A good cook with cheerful disposition was a great help to any riverboat captain; he kept the crew contented and happy. Gordon furnished Bill with everything he asked for, because he knew it would be put to good use, and every meal Bill put on the table was nothing but excellent.

Bill was busy preparing chicken for the crew's supper; George was peeling potatoes; and there was an extra person working in the kitchen that day—Frenchy, donned in white apron and hat was mixing batter for the cornbread.

"I see you have an extra helper today," the captain said to Bill.

Bill laughed. "He insisted on helpin', so I put 'im to work. And Cap'n... you should think about keepin' 'im around."

"I'll take it into consideration," the captain smiled, and then went on about his usual daily inspection. But his thoughts that afternoon were more about Charlie Martin. He knew how much the boy had come to love the river, and his life now seemed to be centered on it and the boat and rafting. It pained Gordon to think that Charlie was going to be taken away from all this that he so dearly enjoyed.

By the second day it was perfectly acceptable to everyone that Charlie ate supper with Captain Gordon at the Officers' table that night, and every other night from then on. They all knew by then that this was Charlie's last trip down the river, and that when they returned to La Crosse, that would be the last they would ever see of him.

It was also accepted that his best friend, Frenchy, was on board for the trip, and it was even rumored that he might become a permanent member of the crew. Captain Gordon avoided any comment on the subject when asked, even though he, too, was starting to admire the boy just a little, if for no other reason than his display of enthusiastic energy.

When there was no opportunity to help in the galley,

and it was Frank McIntyre's watch at the wheel, Frenchy politely asked the pilot, "Would it be okay, M'sieur Frank, if I stayed here in the pilothouse with you for a while?"

"Well, certainly," Frank replied. "You can stay here for as long as you want."

An hour or more passed while Frenchy asked all sorts of questions about the river and steamboats and rafting, and Frank did his best to supply the answers. Frank McIntyre had known the boy for quite some time, but because of his higher social status as a pilot, only now was their friendship beginning to bud.

"Captain Gordon doesn't like me very much, does he?" the boy asked Frank.

"Why do you say that?"

"Because M'sieur Gordon hardly ever talks to me, and he looks at me as if I am odd."

"Oh, I wouldn't worry 'bout it, Frenchy. Cap'n just takes a little more time getting to know somebody. You'll see. By the time we get to Clinton in a few days, he'll treat you just like the rest of us."

"You really think so, M'sieur Frank?"

Frank put his hand on Frenchy's shoulder and winked. "I know so, *mon ami.*"

The boy looked up at Frank and smiled. Their friendship was sealed.

# Chapter 35

*T*he next afternoon the *Bella Mac* was tied up at Dubuque, cooling down the boilers so they could be cleaned. Louis and his crew of eight were busy stowing all the lines and gear after separating the log portion of the raft at the Dubuque mill. David had obtained clear receipts and he was just returning from town after sending a telegram to La Crosse. The boiler cleaning process would take several hours, so Captain Gordon and Frank McIntyre went into town for a break from the routine as well.

Bill shouted down from the galley door on the boiler deck, "Charlie!"

Charlie looked up from the coil of rope he was securing and waved.

"Will ya go with George in the skiff t' th' Boat Store?" Bill called out.

Charlie looked to Louis for his approval. Louis nodded.

"I'll be right there," Charlie called to Bill, and set out for the stairs. On his way, Frenchy caught up to him.

"May I go too, mon ami? I will help row the skiff."

"Sure, you can go," Charlie replied. "I'd be disappointed if you didn't."

When they got to the galley door, Bill handed George his list; George had already gotten money from the clerk. "Now, yer gonna be bringin' back some ice blocks," Bill told them. "So don't dawdle. I'd like to see some ice left when ya git back, okay?"

Charlie and George smiled and giggled; they knew Bill

was just having fun with them about dawdling.

The skiff was still in the water tied to the guard after its use in delivering the logs that afternoon. The boys jumped in, took up the oars and rowed upstream along the shore to the Boat Store. It was similar to the McDonald's store at La Crosse, and just as busy. They waited their turn until a store clerk helped Charlie and Frenchy get the four blocks of ice and the crate of twelve dozen eggs into the skiff. George watched, feeling a little left-out and perhaps a little jealous of Frenchy. Since Frenchy had started helping in the galley, George had developed animosity toward him, worried that Bill wanted to replace him with the new kid. And Frenchy could definitely sense the hostility.

The trip back to the Bella Mac would have been easy and uneventful had it not been for the most vicious wasp that began circling and finally picked George in the middle of the boat as its attack victim. As the bee homed in on him, making several practice dives at the boy, George screamed curses vile enough to strip paint off a church and stood up, flailing his arms in an attempt to fight off the buzzing creature, but only making the bee more angry. Frenchy and Charlie watched this from either end of the skiff, trying to be serious, but they had to laugh. It all seemed quite humorous until George lost his balance and in an instant toppled overboard into the Mississippi. The wasp flew off, having won the battle without firing a single shot.

But George didn't come up out of the dark water.

"Can he swim?" asked Frenchy.

"I don't know," replied Charlie. "Maybe not."

Without any further contemplation, Frenchy quickly

slipped off his clothes and dove into the cold, dark water. Charlie could see neither of them in the murky depths until the sudden eruption of their two heads blasted above the surface, about twenty feet downstream from the boat. Frenchy's left arm was wrapped around George's chest; George's arms were still waving, and he was coughing and gasping for air.

"Row the boat this way," yelled Frenchy.

Charlie put his two oars in the water and pulled hard. When he got close to the boys in the water, he back-paddled a couple of times and then leaned over the side to help George into the boat. He flopped onto the skiff's floor like a fish, still coughing and gasping. Once Charlie was certain he was okay, he said, "Can't swim?"

George shook his head and managed a raspy "No."

"Little Otter will teach you," Charlie said with a grin, and then he took Frenchy's hand and pulled him into the boat.

"Who is *Little Otter?*" George wheezed.

"The fellow who just saved you from drowning. Ain't you gonna thank him?"

George stared at naked and dripping-wet, shivering Frenchy. He sat up, and just a little smile came to his lips. "Thanks," he said quietly. "But you better put your clothes back on now."

The skiff had drifted on the current and was now beside the Bella Mac, with at least half the crew staring at them and cheering from the main deck. But Frenchy didn't mind; George was safe and alive.

# *Chapter 36*

---

*A*t most they were two days away from Clinton, the final destination. Barring any delays or bad weather, Frank calculated the Bella Mac's arrival back in La Crosse after delivering the remaining lumber raft in plenty of time for Easter Sunday. His sister, Mrs. Wood, had a wonderful dinner planned for that day, with Frank and the entire Gordon family as her guests. Frank hoped that Charlie's departure would not occur until after the holiday, so that they might all enjoy one last celebration together.

"LIGHT OFF... WARM UP!" was the call from Captain Gordon when the boiler work was finished. They would run all night, once the steam was up. Double-tripping through the bridges—splitting the raft in half lengthwise and taking each half through the bridge separately, because the whole raft was too wide to fit between the bridge pilings—would not be necessary from there to Clinton. Half of this raft was already gone, so everyone was quite optimistic for an easy trip the rest of the way.

Charlie and Frenchy leaned shoulder to shoulder against the railing on the boiler deck after supper that night, overlooking the bow and the raft of lumber stretching out ahead of the Bella Mac. Twilight was past and darkness had swallowed the river and everything around it. All the birds had left the sky empty and quiet, and now, only the beam of the search light pierced through the misty night air, bouncing from shore to shore as the pilot pointed out landmarks for the oarsmen at the raft's bow.

Some of the off-duty men had gathered on the raft. In keeping with tradition, rafters made their own entertainment, usually in the form of song and dance, and if they were lucky, at least one of the crew was a fiddler or played a banjo.

"So, how do you like the trip so far?" Charlie asked.

"Oh, it is magnifique, mon ami," Frenchy replied. "I have never been such a long way from Barron's Island."

"And it doesn't bother you to be so far away from home?"

"But we will be home again in just a few more days. *Pas du tout...* it does not trouble me at all. And I think I would like to do this always."

"You probably will."

"What do you mean?"

"You can take my place when I'm gone."

"So, it is true, then?" Frenchy said. "You are going away?"

"Like I told you before, Frenchy... I would rather die than leave all this—and you. But I guess I don't have a choice."

Frenchy put his arm firmly around Charlie's shoulders. "I will miss you, more than my brothers."

Down on the raft there seemed to be an argument brewing between two deckhands, and the others were gathered around in anticipation of a fight, as the two were nose to nose, and fingers poking at each other's chests.

"I will be right back," Frenchy said and hurried off.

Charlie wanted to run down there, too, but he

remained at the railing watching and listening to hear what the two men were arguing about. It seemed like only seconds had passed when Frenchy returned carrying his shiny flute. He put it to his lips, took a deep breath, and within moments a lively tune that resembled an Irish jig filled the night air. He had heard the song on the wharf one day and learned to play it flawlessly while tending the cows. One by one the men on the raft turned their attention to the melody, not knowing at first where it came from, and then the two arguing men gradually lost their aggressiveness, too, and before long they seemed to have forgotten their differences.

The fiddler soon joined in and the rest of the crew slapped and stomped their feet in time to the music; the nightly get-together was restored to the usual joyous affair. Captain watched from the Texas deck.

## Chapter 37

*F*renchy had never been to another town other than La Crosse, so naturally, he felt a little intimidated in this strange new place. Charlie, on the other hand, had walked these streets several times during the previous season when Captain had introduced him to some of the better establishments. And it was to some of these that he would take Frenchy. His best friend deserved the best that this city had to offer.

They had walked a few blocks when Charlie stopped in front of Gunter's Tonsorial Parlor. He thought this was as good a time as any to explain to Frenchy what he had planned. "Now Frenchy... this is where the surprise begins."

Frenchy was still puzzled. He had never been inside a barber shop, much less, a high-class tonsorial parlor. His haircuts, lately, had involved a sharp hunting knife and a self-inflicted compromise to his good looks.

"The rest of the guys and me all chipped in," Charlie explained. "Even the captain contributed some."

"What are you doing?" Frenchy asked.

"We're treating you to the finest, starting with a nice haircut... and then we'll go from there. We're gonna make you look like the fine gentleman that you are."

"You mean, mon ami, I'll get a fancy haircut like yours?"

"Yes, Frenchy. And then we'll get you a nice warm bath, and then we're going next door to the haberdashery for a whole new suit of clothes."

"New clothes? For me?"

"Yes, my friend. New clothes... for you. What d'ya think of that?"

"I have never had new clothes before."

"Well, you will now," Charlie said as he urged his friend through the door.

A little reluctant at first, Frenchy climbed into the barber's chair as he was directed, and then he just listened while Charlie instructed the barber to cut Frenchy's hair the same as his own, and that when the haircut was finished, the boy was to get a deluxe bath in the back room.

When Charlie started to walk away, Frenchy cried out, "Don't leave me here alone, mon ami!"

"I'll be right here," Charlie replied as he sat down in a chair by the front window. He watched as the barber carefully trimmed away the long dark hair, and the beginning of a miraculous transformation.

The first sight of himself in the big mirror was a bit of a shock to Frenchy, but then a little grin slowly crept onto his face and it grew to a smile as wide as Main Street. In a matter of moments he was feeling quite pleased with his new appearance.

The barber directed them through a doorway into another comfortable parlor where a bathtub filled with warm water awaited Frenchy.

"Now, let's get those ragged old clothes off, and you can enjoy a nice hot bath," Charlie said.

Frenchy stared at him, and then at the bathtub, seeming a little hesitant.

"It'll be okay, Frenchy," Charlie assured him. "You'll love it."

Frenchy disrobed as instructed and cautiously stepped into the bath. The warm water was soothing and the soap felt good as it slid over his skin. He hadn't had a bath like this since before his mother died. It was magnificent.

When the bath was finished and Frenchy was dry, Charlie wrapped a robe around him. They went out a back door into an alley, and then into the haberdasher's shop. The clerk there remembered Charlie, as he had been there many times with Captain Gordon getting new shirts and trousers.

"I want to buy a complete suit of clothes for my friend," Charlie told the clerk. "Make him look like a fine gentleman."

The clerk looked Frenchy up and down, covered with nothing but the robe from the bath parlor next door. "Undergarments, as well?" he asked.

"Everything," replied Charlie. "Hat and shoes, too."

The clerk wrapped a tape measure around Frenchy's waist, and then he peeled the robe back from his shoulders to get a better look at the boy's build. Then he disappeared for only a minute, returning with the undergarments. "Put these on," he said, "while I see what I have in your size."

Charlie looked on and reminisced about his own similar experience when he first came to Captain Gordon's home. He was delighted that he could do this for Frenchy. And he hoped it would serve as a long-lasting remembrance of their friendship.

# Chapter 38

*F*renchy's own mother would not have recognized the dapper young gent who emerged from the haberdasher's front door, his step a little more confident, his smile brighter than Charlie had seen on him since their fishing days on the La Crosse riverbanks. Charlie walked proudly beside him, a wonderful sense of satisfaction pouring over him like a waterfall. It was sad to think that he would soon be leaving his friend behind.

"If I write you letters, will you promise to answer them?" he asked Frenchy.

Frenchy stopped so suddenly that Charlie had taken three strides before he realized his companion was not beside him.

"Mon ami. Do you forget? I cannot read or write," Frenchy said with a frown.

"Oh, yeah." But then as a revelation Charlie said, "Charlie Martin will teach you!"

They both grinned and walked on toward the river. When they arrived at the Bella Mac, none of the crew was there to greet them. Only James Tulley, the Chief Engineer came strolling up the deck from the engine room. "If you're lookin' fer Captain Gordon," he called out, thinking he was talking to strangers, "he's up..." Then he noticed who the pair was. "Well, well, well! Look at you! Ain't you a sight fer sore eyes?" He turned to Charlie. "Your Pop's up talkin' to David."

"Thanks, Jim," said Charlie and they headed up the stairs to the boiler deck. When they reached the clerk's office, Charlie tapped on the open door. "Hi, Cap'n... David. Where's everybody?"

David looked up at the pair standing in the doorway and smiled. Captain Gordon looked up and frowned. "Where's Frenchy?" he inquired.

"Beg your pardon, M'sieur," the boy replied. "I *am* Frenchy."

By association with the distinct voice and upon closer inspection, he finally recognized the boy, and he was truly amazed. It was quite remarkable; in white shirt with collar, fashionable brown suit and vest, Derby hat and shiny new shoes, Frenchy looked every bit the most refined gentleman as anyone the captain had ever laid eyes on.

Charlie noticed a little smile come onto Captain's face. "Well, Cap'n? What d'ya think?"

Captain looked Frenchy up and down, thinking back on the time when he first saw Charlie with his new clothes and fresh haircut. This transformation seemed even more remarkable. "I think you have done nothing short of miraculous," he replied.

"So, where's all the crew?" Charlie asked. "I'm sure they want to see the *new* Frenchy, too."

The clerk offered an explanation. "There was a little disagreement over wages," David said. "I received a wire from La Crosse instructing me how much to pay the mate's crew, and after they discussed it among themselves, they decided the pay was too low, so they all walked off together."

"They quit? Just like that?"

"It happens a lot this early in the season," the clerk went on. "They're a good bunch, though. This is just their way of bargaining. We'll probably see them back again in a couple of weeks."

"Two weeks!" Charlie whined. He was disappointed that he wouldn't get to say good-bye, and he so wanted to show off Frenchy to them.

"They will be here to see us off," Captain said. "You can say your good-byes then. Besides... they have agreed that two of them will be coming with us so we have enough men to cover the watches on the return trip to La Crosse."

# Chapter 39

*W*hen the *Bella Mac* steamed away from Clinton, six of the mate's crew waved from the riverbank.  They had all said their good-byes to Charlie, and they had all admired Frenchy's dazzling appearance.  Only Will McCannish and Swift Bell remained on board, as agreed, to fill out the needed number for the return trip to La Crosse.

Monday morning found the *Bella Mac* at the Dubuque levee for coal, some grocery supplies and ice, and there had been a request to pick up a passenger.  The Chief Engineer's brother, Henry Tulley, also an engineer, was on his way to La Crosse to join the crew aboard the *Helen Mar*.  And while the coal was being loaded, John Nolan, another old river fireman from New Orleans working his way north, approached the First Mate seeking a ride to La Crosse.  As this crew was short a few members there was plenty of room, and Louis could see no reason to deny the request.

Any other time, Charlie Martin would have been in high spirits on the return trip upriver.  But this was to be his last.  Even though his best friend was there with him, he couldn't help feeling a little sad.  Frenchy was his real salvation; he encouraged Charlie to view his future as a new beginning, and to hope and expect something even better, although neither of them could imagine anything better than what they had now.

Captain recognized Charlie's depression; he sincerely wished he could alter the coming chain of events that would take Charlie away. But he had already changed that course by convincing Mr. Henderson to allow Charlie one more river trip, and there was little chance of expecting any more.

Charlie tried to make the best of his last trip, savoring every moment of enjoyment. Not all of the crew expected his usual level of enthusiasm, but he refused to let his crewmates down, and fully executed his duties as usual.

"Why don't you spend your time with Frenchy?" asked Swift Bell one afternoon. He leaned on the railing beside Charlie, casually scanning the Iowa hills, never making eye contact with Charlie. "He speaks highly of you, and he will be very sad when you go away."

As much as Charlie was aware, Swift Bell was the one person that knew Frenchy's Winnebago heritage, for he was dark-skinned like the boy, and they seemed to have an unspoken understanding of each other. Perhaps the other crewmen knew, as well, but they never commented about it, and Charlie was quite certain that Frenchy's concern of public knowledge about his Indian family should be nothing to worry about.

"I will," Charlie replied. "But I think he's helping Cookie in the galley now. He really likes to do that. He's a great cook, y' know? He learned it from his mother."

"Yes, I knew Morning Star. She was a fine woman."

"You *knew* Frenchy's mother?"

"Sure, I knew her. And it is too bad that she is gone. Frenchy is a fine boy, and he deserves better than losing his whole family the way he did."

Suddenly Charlie realized that he shared information with Swift Bell that only they knew. "I swore to Frenchy a long time ago that I would take to my grave what he told me about his Indian family. He doesn't want everybody to know, but you do."

"Yes, I know. And for Frenchy's peace of mind, I hope you keep your promise to him.

# Chapter 40

*T*hey had made good time going upriver; by Thursday night the *Bella Mac* was only a few hours away from homeport, and they would be home in plenty of time to enjoy the Easter holiday.

"Well, Frank... it's officially Good Friday," said Captain Gordon when he relieved the pilot just after midnight.

"Yes," Frank McIntyre replied. "Everything is running smooth. Monahan is your engineer. We should be in La Crosse by two o'clock. Think I'll try to get a couple hours of sleep."

"Okay, Frank. And I'm really looking forward to that Easter Sunday dinner at your sister's house."

Charlie couldn't sleep, so he had stayed up with Frenchy in their stateroom, reminiscing all the good times they had spent together, truly memorable experiences that would stay with them always. Even at their young age, they understood the importance of their friendship. But this was a difficult time for both, as their companionship neared an end. Charlie's future was uncertain, and he was uneasy knowing that all the familiar surroundings and his entire life was about to change. He wished Frenchy could come with him to New York, but he knew that was impossible. And he knew that Frenchy was going to be happy in his new-found career aboard a riverboat, providing that Captain could convince some other boat master in need of a cook to hire him.

About midnight, Frenchy's eyes were beginning to get heavy and his head nodded. *"J'ai besoin de dormir,"* he mumbled.

Charlie stared at his friend questioningly.

"I need to go to sleep," Frenchy explained, realizing that in his tired state, he had spoken words that Charlie didn't understand.

"It's time for me to go to work, anyway," Charlie said. "I'll see you in the morning."

*"Bonsoir, mon ami."* Frenchy's eyes were already closed.

But Charlie didn't go directly to the main deck; he left the stateroom and made his way forward; he climbed the stairs to the Texas deck to have a chat with Captain in the pilothouse first.

"Hi, Cap'n," he said. Frank McIntyre had just retired to his stateroom to sleep until they reached La Crosse, and Gordon was alone with the river and his searchlight.

"Well, hello, Charlie." He put one arm around the boy's shoulders. He, too, was fighting the urge to cry whenever he thought about Charlie leaving.

Charlie just stood there for a few minutes watching the light beam reflecting off the water and dancing along the riverbanks as Captain expertly maneuvered the craft where the channel crossed to the west shoreline. They were a few miles below Brownsville, and Charlie recognized the little island where he and Frenchy had camped the first night of what Captain had considered their "unauthorized lark" a few years before. But he decided not to mention it, because it might stir up a reason to be scolded once again for something that happened so long ago.

"I was thinking," Charlie said. "D'ya s'pose you could find Frenchy a job on a riverboat?"

"Well, I don't know..." There seemed to be a little skepticism in Captain's voice.

"He's really a good cook, y' know. And he really likes being on a riverboat. He told me."

By this time, Captain had begun to recognize Frenchy's likeability, and he knew the boy had sound, positive character, but he wasn't yet assured of his ability as a faithful and reliable crewman. "I'll take it into consideration," he said, and then, as if avoiding further conversation on that subject he peered at the steam pressure gauge. It showed the normal 135 pounds, but the boat seemed sluggish and slow. He thought, perhaps, that it was his imagination, only because he was anxious to get home.

Charlie saw that he wasn't going to get a better answer than that right then. "I'd better get down to the main deck," he said, "and see what there is for me to do."

As he left the pilothouse, Captain said to him quietly, "We'll talk about it some more at home, okay?"

Charlie smiled, nodded, and sprinted down the stairs.

# Chapter 41

"*W*ake up, you good fer nothin' dog," Charlie heard the fireman, Maurice Leseur calling out. He soon learned that the fireman was trying to arouse the engineer, Charles Monahan. Monahan had taken over the engine room duties from Chief Engineer Jim Tulley a couple of hours earlier. Now he was leaned back in his chair snoozing, apparently blocking the fireman from checking his boiler fires. With all the cursing from Monahan for Maurice disturbing his nap, Charlie left them to their differences, strolled to the bow, and watched the searchlight brighten the very dark night, briefly here, briefly there, like lightning before a storm. After a few minutes he wandered to the stern and listened to the slow rhythm of the paddlewheel churning the dark water. It was a sound that he knew he would not hear again once the boat landed at La Crosse.

Up at the boilers, Monahan and Leseur had discovered trouble. The "doctor" as it was called—the steam driven pump that supplied water to the boilers—had stopped operating. A pipe flange fitting had worked loose, and steam pressure to the pump had dropped, causing the pump to stop, the very reason that was causing Captain Gordon his frustrations with the slowness of the boat. He kept signaling to the engineer, but Monahan was too busy trying to remedy the leaking pipe to respond. Eventually he was successful with the repair, and the doctor resumed its operation, but by that time the water level in the boilers was dangerously low. Cold river water poured into the overheated boilers, and they soon emitted an eerie moan. Monahan recognized the imminent danger; he panicked and ran from the boilers to the far stern, Leseur right on his heels.

Their abrupt actions startled Charlie. The fear in their eyes told him that something dreadful was about to happen. He processed the thought about as quickly as they explained the situation. "Then we have to stop the pump!" He darted toward the boilers before Leseur could catch his arm to hold him back. "It's too late for that," Leseur yelled, still attempting to catch the boy, but young Charlie was too fast for him and kept a few strides ahead. He had learned enough about steamboats to know the consequences; cold water pumped into an overheated boiler could result in an explosion, the force of which could destroy the entire boat, and he intended to save the boat from destruction.

About half-way Charlie found himself on a sandy beach; it was cool and pleasant, and waving to him stood a man dressed in a military uniform, much older than him, but he looked just like Charlie. He was either far in the past or far in the future, and one of them had to be terribly out of place.

Captain Gordon miraculously escaped serious injury as he was catapulted through the front window of the pilothouse, landing on the bow deck, completely disoriented. In his dazed state, he got to his feet and immediately discovered his right foot would not entirely support his weight. He touched his face that stung from cuts, and even in the darkness, without seeing the red on his hand, he knew he was bleeding.

Nothing made sense to him. It was as if he had been launched suddenly into a nightmare. But slowly his senses began to revive, and he realized that he was no longer at the wheel in the pilothouse, and he was not gazing at the river ahead in the beam of the searchlight. As his eyes gradually adjusted to the darkness, he sensed the total destruction all around him, and everything was deathly quiet.

Then he remembered that he had been talking with Charlie in the pilothouse that seemed like just moments ago, but it may have been longer. He didn't know how long he had been unconscious.

Charlie. He had to find Charlie.

# Chapter 42
## Good Friday April 7, 2:15 a.m.

*A* thunderous rumble awoke the residents in the little river town of Brownsville, Minnesota, the report so violent that it shook houses and rattled windows and sent sleepy dogs under porches fearful of the unknown cause of the tremor. But some people recognized the horrendous boom; Cy Alexander, an old retired Mississippi pilot had ears like a hawk when it came to river sounds. He had been awake and heard *Bella Mac's* whistle, recognizing the distinct tone. And then, a few minutes later the sickening boom shook his house and rattled the dishes in the cupboard. He knew immediately that *Bella Mac's* boilers had exploded; it was a sound he knew all too well. He bolted out of his chair and rushed to the front door. Outside in the cool April air he discovered that other people had come out of their houses, curious of the noise and what had made their homes tremble.

Out of the darkness they could hear distressed voices calling out for help. "Bring out a skiff!" came shouts from the vicinity of Two Mile Island, just upriver from Brownsville. Alexander understood the urgency, because he knew what had happened. There was bound to be loss of life, and no doubt, there would be injured men on a sinking boat who needed help.

He hurried to his neighbor's house to get some able-bodied help. Frantically he pounded on the door. "John! Wake up! I need your help!"

John Reppy opened the door, sleepy-eyed but alert enough to recognize Alexander and his urgent request. "What kinda help d'ya need?" he asked, rubbing his eyes.

"I think it's the *Bella Mac*. Her boilers blew. They're calling for help out there."

"Where?"

"Sounds like they're up by Two Mile Island. Get dressed. Hurry! We can row out in a skiff."

In another part of town not far away, Elijah Palmer and his brother George heard the explosion. Elijah had a faint suspicion of its origin. He and George rushed outside where they could hear the mournful cries for help piercing through the dark night from out on the river: *"Bring a skiff. Bring a skiff."*

They responded as quickly as possible and rowed out into the darkness, seeing very little, following only the sounds of distressed voices. By the time they reached the steamer, its wreckage had floated downstream on the current quite some distance from where the disaster had occurred. Without lanterns and no lights remaining operational on the big boat, they could only imagine the destruction by the gruesome silhouette lying in the water. Only a small portion of the upper deck just ahead of the paddlewheel remained intact; the rest of the structure had been reduced to a pile of splintered rubble piled on the hull, or blown out of existence, or scattered about the river's surface from the blast.

When they neared the wreckage, a boy's face appeared, and he seemed to have in tow another man, who Elijah and George helped into the boat. The boy momentarily vanished in the darkness, and then reappeared with another injured man. They helped him and the boy into the skiff. All three looked as though they had been tossed from their beds into the river wearing nothing but their undergarments, speechless from exhaustion and the shock of such a violent awakening.

Rowing vigorously, Elijah and George delivered the three rescued crewmen to shore. By then there were many Brownsville residents waiting at the landing ready to help the victims in any way they could.

Cy Alexander and John Reppy returned to the landing with two more crewmen, one of which they had given up for dead. They had found him afloat, still on a bunk in the wreckage of what remained of a stateroom. The other had been clinging to a large broken beam. He was too incoherent to even say his name.

Alexander caught one bystander by his arm. With authority in his voice he said, "Go to the telegraph office at the railroad depot and have the operator send an *urgent* message to the McDonalds in La Crosse. It's the *Bella Mac* out there. Her boilers exploded. Some dead. Many injured. Hurry!" Then as an afterthought he added, "And be sure to tell the operator to ask for more medical assistance."

Charles Billings and Joseph Williams, another pair of Brownsville residents arrived at the landing with two more survivors; they had rescued the Tulley brothers, Henry and James who they found hanging onto a piece of timber. They had been propelled from their bunks into the water, but neither were injured any worse than they could swim to the safety of the floating beam.

## *Chapter 43*

*B*y then the river was alive with rescue boats manned by Brownsville residents eager to help. When Elijah and George Palmer made it back out to the wrecked steamer they found it marooned on the Wisconsin side of the river against the bank, its hull filled with water. They could hear a frantic voice calling: "Charlie! Charlie! Is that you?"

Another muffled voice answered: "No. It's me, Louis."

Aboard what was left of the *Bella Mac*, Captain Gordon had climbed upon what appeared to be remnants of the upper deck, atop a heap of splintered boards and beams. He could hear the First Mate's voice below his feet. Louis was buried under the wreckage. With blood dripping from his chin and a foot that felt like it was on fire, the Captain started pulling broken boards and timbers from the mound of rubble. "I'll get you out of there," he said to Louis.

"You okay, Cap'n?" another voice said from the darkness. It was Bill Wagner, a fireman, apparently not injured too severely, and Gordon was glad to hear his voice. After much great difficulty and pain, they finally lifted the beam that had Louis pinned down.

As they helped Louis to his feet, they heard a crashing noise. They didn't know then, but they would soon learn that the crash was a falling stove, and its still-burning contents spilled out among the rubble. The kindling-like material quickly ignited, and now they faced another crisis; the boat would soon be ablaze.

From nearby, Louis could hear a sorrowful moaning. "Cap'n! I hear someone!"

Gordon listened. He, too, heard the moan. "Charlie! Is that you?" he called out, but the only response was another moan.

They followed the sound to the outer edge of the hull. Barely hanging on to the gunwale was the badly injured fireman, Maurice Leseur. Louis and Gordon pulled Maurice up onto the deck but he could not speak more than grunts and groans.

"We'll take him in our skiff," Elijah Palmer offered. His voice startled Captain Gordon, but he was relieved to know that assistance was at hand.

George and Elijah lifted the fireman into their skiff. "Anybody else we can take to shore?"

"Haven't found any more, yet," Bill Wagner replied. "Better take Maurice now... looks like he's hurt pretty bad."

"Charlie!" the Captain called out again, and limped toward the stern of the crippled boat.

"Maybe Charlie is one of them we already took to Brownsville," Elijah called out to him.

"A blond-haired boy? About eighteen?"

"There was a boy," Elijah said, and then started rowing across the channel.

"Help me now, boys," came a cry from under the heap of debris. "Da faar is gettin' close," the voice called out. It was Tommy Rice, the only black deckhand.

"Try to find a bucket," Gordon yelled to the First Mate. "I can see Tommy in the light of the fire."

Gordon and Wagner went frantically to work pulling

twisted timbers and splintered wood away from where the deckhand was trapped. The flames were reaching his legs that were caught under several broken beams and tangled in cables. "Thow s'm wata on dat faar!" Tommy said. "M' laigs is burnin' up."

"This is all I could find," said Louis returning with a broken wooden bucket. "But it'll hold water, and it'll hafta do!" He went to the edge of the deck, dipped the bucket full of water and handed it to Wagner, who in turn passed it to Gordon. He dashed the water on the flames, but it did little to subdue the fire. He passed the bucket back, and a few moments later it returned to him full. Again he tried to douse the flames while Wagner attempted to remove some more debris, but the fire raged on.

Now there were more men climbing onto the vessel from skiffs, rushing in to help pass the water bucket. Another wooden bucket was located, and the fire fighting progressed. But when the flames were extinguished, Tommy's legs were badly burned. He had passed out from the pain by the time they extricated him from the rubble and put him in a skiff.

"Charlie!" Captain Gordon called out again, and once more he set out in search of his son. Only a few steps resulted in a fall when he tried to support himself on the injured foot. Bill Wagner came to his aid. "We'll look for Charlie," he said. "You go in a skiff to the landing. You're bleeding, and you need medical attention. We'll take care of things here."

Captain sat there for a moment, weak, discouraged, defeated. His boat was destroyed; his son was missing; and he was losing a lot of blood. He accepted help from one of the rescuers into a rowboat where he sat and watched his wonderful *Bella Mac* slowly receded into the darkness as the skiff moved across the river to Brownsville.

Lights brightened windows in nearly every house in the village, and the residents were eagerly willing to shelter the injured victims that were brought, one by one to the houses. The only physician in the village, Dr. Riley, kept busy, going from house to house administering first aid, and determining which ones needed more attention. Some were beyond his help.

"What's your name, son?" the doctor asked of the young man at Sonja Johnson's house. It was his first test of every patient from the boat to determine if they were coherent.

"Dominic Bouton, M'sieur," he responded. "But everyone calls me Frenchy." He was shivering from spending a considerable length of time in the cold river water, and Mrs. Johnson had wrapped a blanket around him. "My new clothes," Frenchy cried. "I have lost my new clothes." Tears streamed down his cheeks. It wasn't the clothes that concerned him most—it was that Charlie had given them to him, and they held more significance to him than just garments.

"We'll find your clothes," Dr. Riley said. "But right now, let me take a look at you. Do you have any severe pains?"

Frenchy stood and pulled back the blanket to show the doctor bruises and scrapes on his stomach and thighs, but there didn't seem to be any broken bones or bleeding wounds that required immediate attention.

"You're mighty lucky, Frenchy," the doctor said. "You must've been at the stern when the boilers exploded."

"Oui, M'sieur. I was asleep...our room was the very last one at the back of the boat. But how do you know that, M'sieur?"

"Because you're not burned. All the others who were farther toward the bow... above the boilers... were scalded by the steam."

Frenchy clutched the little pendant medicine bag that still hung at his chest, and he recalled what his uncle had told him—that *it would protect him from thunder in the night.* But he said nothing of that to the doctor. He only asked about his friend. "What about Charlie Martin? Have you seen him yet?"

"No one by that name," the doctor replied as he prepared to move on to the next patient. "I'll send over some ointment to put on those scrapes."

Chris Gerhardt was escorting the doctor to the houses where the *Bella Mac* victims had been taken and he was waiting at the door. "Chris," Dr. Riley said. "Send word down to the boys at the landing to try to find some clothes on that boat. All these men need their clothes... that is, if there are any left to find."

# Chapter 44

*H*elen was already in the kitchen baking bread in anticipation of the Captain's and Charlie's arrival. She heard a knock at the door. Certainly *they* wouldn't knock, and it seemed a bit odd for anyone to be visiting at such an early hour. The clock had just chimed five.

"Hi, Helen. Sorry to bother you so early," the messenger said. "But I have an urgent message from the McDonalds."

Helen's smiling face turned solemn. An *urgent message* at this hour could not be good news. "What is it?" she asked. She could sense the young man's troubled feelings. He had been there many times delivering messages to Captain Gordon, but this time she knew something was amiss.

"The *Bella Mac's* boilers exploded early this morning down at Brownsville."

The housekeeper had lived in the midst of a river man long enough to know what that meant. "Oh, dear. Is the Captain...?" She couldn't bring herself to speak the rest of the question.

"We don't know the fate of all those aboard, yet. Alex

and Charles McDonald are taking another boat down there. The telegram said *'many injured'* and they've been brought ashore and are being cared for at Brownsville homes."

Tears welled up in Helen's eyes. "I'll wake Maria and have James drive us down to the boatyard."

"Yes, ma'am. That would be a good idea."

News of *Bella Mac's* misfortune spread quickly throughout La Crosse in those early morning hours after the telegraph message from Brownsville arrived. Intense anxiety rose as it was known that many La Crosse men were on that boat. Friends and families of crewmen were already gathered at the boatyard just north of Clinton Street when Alex and Charles McDonald, owners of the *Bella Mac,* arrived at six o'clock accompanied by Dr. McArthur. None of the McDonald's boats were available, but the *Alfred Toll,* a raft boat owned by rival P.S. Davidson, lay in the harbor with steam built up and ready to sail. This was no time to think about rivalry. The *Alfred Toll's* crew didn't hesitate to assist, and not a moment was lost to point the steamer downriver.

Sam Henderson was among the onlookers as they watched the boat pull away. He had been eating his breakfast at the Bellevue Hotel when he overheard a messenger inform the clerk that there would be injured crewmen from a riverboat accident brought there, so the hotel could prepare for their arrival.

"What boat?" the clerk asked.

"The *Bella Mac*... her boilers exploded near Brownsville."

Henderson recognized the name and a cold chill raced down his spine. Although he hadn't lived his life in a river town, he had read plenty of news reports of steamboat boiler explosions, and he was well aware of the destruction and injury—and death—they could cause. Reginald Van Hugh III was aboard that boat, and suddenly he was angry with himself for allowing Captain Gordon to take the boy on one last trip.

By nine o'clock there had been no word from Brownsville. Newspaper reporters, among many other curious citizens and anxious families, wanted to go to the scene. But the southbound train to Dubuque had suffered engine problems and was running quite late, so getting to Brownsville by rail was out of the question. No other means of conveyance presented itself. One reporter for the *Republican Leader* grew more impatient as the minutes ticked by; he needed his story for the afternoon edition. Recruiting the help of a couple of old experienced river men he knew, they set out in a skiff. After an hour of vigorous rowing they could see the *Alfred Toll* and another freight boat, the *Vigor,* at the Brownsville landing, but they pointed their skiff to the site of the forlorn remains of the *Bella Mac* beached on the Wisconsin shore nearly opposite the village. Hardly anything remained to suggest that this pile of rubble was once a riverboat—only the paddlewheel and a small portion of the rear cabin. The rest looked like a disorderly stack of kindling on the sunken hull, a demoralizing sight.

A number of men from Brownsville were busy searching through the rubble on the main deck for the missing crew members thought to be buried under the debris. So far, they had only found one body that now lay on the forward deck covered with a quilt.

"Who's the dead body?" the reporter asked one of the men.

"Don't know for sure. We sent Fred over to give his description to the Captain. He'll prob'ly know."

"So, Captain Gordon is alive?"

"Sure is. He's cut up and limpin' and pretty discouraged, but he seems to be okay."

"All the others over in Brownsville?"

"Them that survived. Some are still missing. We only found the one. The rest prob'ly drowned."

The reporter quickly jotted everything down in his notepad, made a mental sketch of the wreck, and then he and his two assistants rowed across to Brownsville.

# Chapter 45

**A**ll of the *Bella Mac's* surviving crew had been carried or helped aboard the *Alfred Toll*. And now, with the report of the one body found aboard the wreck, eleven of the seventeen were accounted for; six were still missing.

The newspaper reporter approached the *Alfred Toll's* captain on the levee. Reluctantly, permission was granted him to ride back to La Crosse. But before the pilot pointed the steamer upriver, he steered toward the Wisconsin shore to the wreck site. They had a body to retrieve.

As the steamer crossed the channel, a telegraph message was being transmitted to La Crosse: *One dead. Ten injured. Returning to La Crosse now aboard the Alfred Toll.*

The water was deep enough for the boat to pull alongside the sunken hull. Captain Gordon hobbled with a crutch to where three members of the search party were lifting a body wrapped in a quilt onto the deck of the *Alfred Toll*. Two others were transferring stacks of clothing and a few personal belongings they had found in the wreckage.

Whoever was under that quilt, Captain Gordon knew his emotions would overwhelm him, and he tried to prepare for the worst. When the cover was pulled back from the cut and burned face of the victim lying on the deck, Gordon stared a few moments, covered his eyes with one hand and turned away so the others wouldn't see his tears.

Frenchy sat next to the bunk where Maurice Leseur laid, his entire body scalded and his face and arms bandaged to stop cuts from bleeding. It was comforting to him to know Frenchy was there. "I tried to stop him," Leseur could barely speak.

The boy leaned closer to hear.

"That brave young fellow was gonna shut down the pump... save us all," Maurice continued. "I tried to stop him... knew it was too late... but he ran too fast for me."

"Who?" Frenchy asked.

"Charlie, mon ami. Charlie." The horribly burned fireman's pain was too intense, and he could say no more.

Bill Wagner came into the room carrying a bundle of clothing. "They found your clothes, Frenchy. Well, most of them anyway." He handed the bundle to the boy, still draped with Mrs. Johnson's blanket. Tears of joy trickled down his cheeks. With the exception of the derby hat and one shoe, his new clothes had been recovered. And equally important, in the bundle was a tattered wooden box, and inside, his cherished flute seemed unharmed.

*"Merci, mon ami,"* Frenchy beamed.


The reporter snuck from room to room where the injured crewmen awaited their arrival at La Crosse. Those who were able gave him their accounts of what had happened to them, but most had been sleeping at the time of the explosion. Their only recollections were of being rescued.

Only the on duty engineer, Charles Monahan, was able to tell him anything about before the boilers exploded. "Everything was running normal," he lied. "Steam pressure was at 135 and a full gauge of water in the boilers. Why they blew is a mystery to me."

But the reporter wondered, if Monahan had been in the midst of the machinery at the time of the explosion, why he wasn't scalded or injured as severely as the others. *That* was a mystery to the reporter.

An enormous crowd had gathered at the La Crosse levee by noon when the *Alfred Toll* landed. Hundreds of voices hushed and only murmurs floated about in speculation as the quilt-wrapped body was carried off the boat and placed in the waiting undertaker's wagon.

One by one the victims of the *Bella Mac* disaster were carried or assisted of the boat, Dr. McArthur directing the assistants to take the badly injured to the Bellevue house where they would all be under one roof for further medical attention. Sadly, he knew he would see some die there.

Captain Gordon was the last to leave the boat. He had stayed behind to see that everyone of his crew was safely on shore. As he approached, Dr. McArthur was instructing the blanket-clad Frenchy to follow the men who were taking the badly injured to the hotel.

"No," Captain intervened. "He will come with me. I need his help to get to my carriage."

Frenchy, cradling the bundle of clothes, gazed curiously at the captain.

"I guess that will be okay," said the physician. "His injuries aren't so severe. But I will be to your house later to look after you."

Maria spotted Captain and the boy as they walked toward the carriage. She lifted the hem of her skirt and ran to meet them.

"Oh! Papa!" she cried. "I've been so worried." She

threw her arms around him and hugged him tightly as tears streamed down her face. Then she released her embrace and gazed briefly at Frenchy, on whose shoulder Captain leaned. "Where is Charlie? Is he okay?" Her eyes stared a worrisome look into her father's.

Captain only shook his head, and then nodded toward the hearse that was slowly making its way through the crowd.

"Oh, Papa. No!" Maria bawled uncontrollably. Helen arrived to help her back to the carriage.

"Help young Frenchy into the carriage," Gordon said to his gardener, James. "He will be coming home with us."

# *Chapter 46*
## June 3, 1882

*H*elen was pleased that another boy was there to fill a void in Charlie's absence, especially for Captain's sake. She knew Frenchy had been the one who lured Charlie on that excursion down the river in his canoe, and that he had remained a sore subject with Captain for quite some time after that incident. But that was long ago, and in time, the story had become one of those endeared and humorous memories of the past.

And what a gentleman he was! So appreciative of the bedroom that had been Charlie's, and of all the fine clothes that fit him as if they were custom-made just for him. His manners at the supper table astounded even Maria, until she learned of his upbringing in a home of distinguished French culture. He was eager to learn to read, and Maria enjoyed tutoring him; she would gladly direct her efforts to prepare him for school. It all made missing Charlie less painful.

No longer did he have to tend the cattle on the hillside meadow, and now his beautiful canoe rested out of the weather in the carriage house instead of on the bank of that algae-covered lagoon behind a deteriorating log house on Barron's Island. No longer did he have to hunt rabbits, or prepare venison, or chop firewood to survive through the winter. Being a kind-hearted, caring friend had paid its rewards. But he still missed his best friend.

A knock came at the door. Helen was not surprised to see Andy, the messenger from the McDonald boatyard, as there had been considerable communication with Captain Gordon during his time of convalescence. He no longer needed the crutch, but he still limped noticeably, and the cuts on his face were still healing.

Helen escorted Andy to the den where Captain was having his morning coffee and reading the newspaper.

"Hi, Cap'n," the messenger said. "How are you feeling today?"

"Like an old man with a broken foot and cut lip. What brings you here, Andy?"

"Well, there's been a body found in the river down below Brownsville."

Captain jerked his attention away from the paper and stared at the messenger, waiting for further explanation.

"They think it's one of your lost crewmen from the *Bella Mac*. The McDonalds want you to go down there and identify the body 'cause you knew those men better than anyone. The *Mollie Mohler* packet boat will stop at the Brownsville landing for you and the body on her way upriver this afternoon." He reached in his breast pocket. "Here is your rail ticket to Brownsville. Louis will be at the depot, too. He'll go with you."

Gordon took the ticket and bid Andy a farewell as Helen escorted him back to the door.

This had been a trying time for Gordon: he'd sat through excruciating examinations as government officials investigated the accident. He'd attended more funerals than he cared to think about. And then there was the formal hearing when his Second Engineer, Charles Monahan was charged with carelessness and neglect by sleeping while on duty, and was stripped of his engineer's license. Losing Charlie and his best friend, Frank McIntyre had been the most devastating blow to his morale, and apparently, the nightmare hadn't ended yet.

The body that he and Louis viewed on the levee at Brownsville that day was that of an average sized man, but it was so badly decomposed there was nothing left to identify.

"It's Frank McIntyre," declared Captain Gordon.

Louis, however, wasn't in total agreement. Judging by the plaid flannel shirt and jeans, he thought the remains were Will McCannish, whose two brothers, George and David had been buried nearly two months earlier.

The captain thought for a moment how he would justify his decision. Frank had always been his best friend, and he owed to Frank's sister the end of her grieving, wishing for Frank's decent burial. "Those are the clothes I saw Frank wearing when I relieved him in the pilothouse the last time I saw him alive."

The captain's decision was final, for it was he who had been given the responsibility. When they returned to La Crosse, they visited Mrs. Woods, Frank McIntyre's sister and informed her that they had found her brother.

After the funeral two days later, Captain Gordon limped out to a bench in the garden that was in full bloom. Birds were singing; butterflies flitted about. He hoped it was all over.

On the other side of the wall next to the La Crosse River, Dominic Bouton sat on the bank thinking about a friend.

# *Postscript*

Although it is a work of fiction, this story is based on true historic events. The two main characters, Charlie Martin and Frenchy were real people, as were most of the characters depicted in the story. The *Bella Mac* was an actual riverboat owned by the McDonald Brothers of La Crosse, Wisconsin. Its demise described in this book is factual, according to newspaper accounts that were published by the *La Crosse Republican Leader*, written by surviving crew members, and reporters who saw, first-hand, the wrecked boat and interviewed surviving crew shortly after the catastrophe occurred.

A government investigation of this accident followed and attributed the cause of the boiler explosion to carelessness and neglect by Charles Monahan, second engineer, who was on duty at the time of the blast. His engineer's license was revoked as a result. A total of nine lives were lost. They were:

Swift Bell, deckhand, body never found.

Maurice Leseur, fireman, died Apr. 9, 1882.

Charles Martin, deckhand, adopted son of Captain Gordon, died instantly.

David McCannish, Chief Clerk, died Apr. 10, 1882.

George McCannish, assist. cook, body recovered Apr. 9, 1882.

William McCannish, deckhand, body never found.

Frank McIntyre, Second Pilot, body recovered June 3,

1882.*

John Nolan, fireman, (Not employed on *Bella Mac* but was working his passage upriver) body never found.

Tom Rice, deckhand, died Apr 8, 1882.

*Many years after the *Bella Mac* explosion near Brownsville, Minnesota, and long after the death of Captain Gordon, the last surviving crew member, his First Mate, Louis Suelflohn submitted his story of the incident to the *La Crosse Tribune*.  In comparison, his account was consistent with news reports filed at the time of the accident, but he revealed one fact that had been kept a secret for fifty years.

Mrs. Woods (Frank McIntyre's widowed sister) cared for the grave of a total stranger.  She never learned the truth about the deed committed by close friend, Captain W.W. Gordon, intended as a gesture of compassion.  Many years later, the Captain confidentially acknowledged to Louis Suelflohn that, at the time, he was aware the body he identified on June 3, 1882 at Brownsville was not that of Frank McIntyre.  In answer to the question, "Why, then, did you insist that it was?" he replied, "To satisfy his sister that her brother would have a decent burial."

Only the two of them—Gordon and Suelflohn—were ever aware of the substitution until 1932 when Louis' story was published in the newspaper.

# ABOUT THE AUTHOR

Born into a farm family in the late 1940s, J.L. Fredrick lived his youth in rural Western Wisconsin, a modest but comfortable life not far from the Mississippi River. His father was a farmer, and his mother, an elementary school teacher. He attended a one-room country school for his first seven years of education.

Wisconsin has been home all his life, with exception of a few years in Minnesota and Florida. After college in La Crosse, Wisconsin and a stint with Uncle Sam during the Viet Nam era, the next few years were unsettled as he explored and experimented with life's options. He entered into the transportation industry in 1975.

Since 2001 he has nine published novels to his credit, and one history volume, *Rivers, Roads, & Rails,* a non-fiction account of Midwestern history that focuses on the development of transportation during the pioneer days—steamboats, stagecoaches, and the beginnings of the Midwest's railroads—and the impact they had on the growth and prosperity of Midwest communities. He was a featured author during Grand Excursion 2004.

J.L. Fredrick currently resides at Madison, Wisconsin.